PEN PALS:
SUPER SPECIAL TWO

SUMMER
SIZZLE

by Sharon Dennis Wyeth

A YEARLING BOOK

Published by
Dell Publishing
a division of
Bantam Doubleday Dell Publishing Group, Inc.
666 Fifth Avenue
New York, New York 10103

Copyright © 1991 by Parachute Press, Inc.

All rights reserved. No part of this book may be reproduced or transmitted in any form or by any means, electronic or mechanical, including photocopying, recording or by any information storage and retrieval system, without the written permission of the Publisher, except where permitted by law.

Illustrations by Wendy Wax

The trademark Yearling ® is registered in the U.S. Patent and Trademark Office.
The trademark Dell® is registered in the U.S. Patent and Trademark Office.

ISBN: 0-440-40470-3

Published by arrangement with Parachute Press, Inc.
Printed in the United States of America
June 1991
10 9 8 7 6 5 4 3 2 1
OPM

*For Tasha White and
Carissa Dennis*

To Whoever Finds This Time Capsule:

My name is Shanon Davis, and I live with my suitemates, Maxie Schloss, Amy Ho, and Palmer Durand, in Suite 3-D of Fox Hall. That's why we call ourselves the Foxes of the Third Dimension.

This summer we're at Emerald Lake, a camp in the White Mountains of New Hampshire. And best of all— Camp Emerald is *CO-ED!!!* Alma Stephens (our school) and Ardsley Academy (home of the guys who are our pen pals) rented the space for a summer outdoor program.

This will be the first time we Foxes have had the chance to live this close to a bunch of boys, and you can believe— we're all excited to the max! We're a little nervous, too, but we're absolutely, positively sure that this will be the most wonderful three weeks of our lives.

Which is the reason we decided to write down every single thing that happens and put it in this time capsule— we want to save all this good stuff for the future.

Maxie, Amy, Palmer, and I are going to take turns telling our parts of the story. Since this was all my idea, I get to go first.

Hope you enjoy reading this as much as we did living it!

Shanon Davis
Amy Ho
Maxie Schloss
Palmer Durand

P.S. I don't live in Suite 3-D, but I hang out there a lot because Palmer is my older stepsister. So I think it's only fair that you get my slant on the happenings, too.

Georgette Durand

TIME CAPSULE
ENTRY ONE:
BY SHANON DAVIS

Dearest Shanon,

In case you're wondering why I haven't showed up yet: JEEZ, I BROKE MY KNEES! Actually, only one of my legs is banged up, but I wanted the first part of this sorry story to rhyme.

Two days before I was supposed to leave for camp, I was riding my dirt bike through the patch of woods behind my house when a humongous monster jumped out on the path ahead of me. Okay, so it was only a middle-sized raccoon, but at the time, it looked truly awesome. Anyway, I swerved to avoid it, my bike hit a tree, and just like that, the time I've been looking forward to spending with you and the rest of the gang is history. BUMMER!!

The cast the doctor slapped on me after the accident weighs a ton and I'll be stuck with it for over a month. While you're catching the rays and playing mermaid in the sparkling waters of Emerald Lake, I'll be going bonkers trying to figure out how to get through the plaster to scratch an itch on my shin.

At least you'll still have a terrific time—one of us has to.

*Just don't forget that you're my pen pal. Scratch that—
you're my one-and-only, all-time favorite, best girl!*

*Write soon and let me know all the happenings—
your letters will be the only thing between me and total
boredom.*

Love,
Mars

I stared down at the sheet of paper in my hand, feeling numb. For once there was no comfort in seeing Mars Martinez's familiar, back-slanted handwriting.

"What's up, Shanon?" Maxie Schloss, who'd been my roommate during my second year at Alma Stephens School for Girls, stopped unpacking her gear long enough to shoot me a puzzled glance.

"Mars didn't just miss the bus like we thought he did— he won't be coming to Camp Emerald at all," I croaked miserably.

My announcement put all other activity in the bunk on hold. Maxie came over to sit beside me. Amy Ho left the drawer she was filling with black T-shirts and shorts, and Palmer Durand temporarily abandoned her search for the most comfortable bed among the seven in the room.

Glumly, I passed around the note from Mars.

"He broke his leg?" Amy said in shock.

"What timing," Palmer murmured. She shook her head, showing off her long blond hair. (Palmer does that a lot.) "It's terrific that he wants you to be his girl, but it doesn't do you much good if he's not here."

"I know." The three weeks I'd dreamed about for so long had been trashed by a mangy raccoon.

"I know you're going to miss him, but there are lots of fun things to do here," Amy said. "Saturday evening, there's going to be a canoe ride, and when we get to the island in the middle of the lake, we'll have a sing-along around the campfire."

"Yeah, and while you're watching the sunset and roasting marshmallows with Nikos Smith, I'll be swatting mosquitoes," I predicted.

"Mars's accident is a lousy break—no joke intended—but you shouldn't waste your vacation moping about it," Palmer said. She got up from the bunk and wandered over to stare through the window, a calculating expression creeping into her blue eyes. "There are at least a hundred Grade-A Ardies roaming around out there. Just cut one out of the herd and go for him."

In spite of being totally depressed, I almost giggled; the "love-the-one-you're-with" M.O. was so typically Palmer. Although the last part of her advice didn't work for me, she was right about one thing: I couldn't spend the next three weeks feeling sorry for myself. Straightening my shoulders, I forced myself to smile. "This has to be a lot worse for Mars than it is for me—at least I'm not stuck with a heavy cast. I'll make something in crafts, and I'll write every day so he won't feel left out."

"Good plan," Amy said. "You can keep a log of everything we do."

"Better still, you could use Mr. Griffith's camcorder to make a videotape," Maxie added. "Even if you can't be with Mars, you know how much he cares about you. I wish . . ."

Maxie's voice trailed off and I knew from the wistful look on her face that she was thinking about her own pen pal, Paul Grant. Even though Maxie wouldn't admit it, I knew she was crazy about him, and I suspected the feeling was mutual. It was kind of weird, though. When they were together, they mumbled a lot and spent most of their time trying not to look at each other. Maybe while we were here, they'd get over some of their shyness.

"So," I said, determined to stop feeling depressed. "Why are we sitting here yakking? Let's finish unpacking so we can start having fun!"

"We're going to need more storage space," Palmer complained, tugging one of the bags from her amazing pile of luggage.

"You brought enough clothes for the entire camp," Maxie observed good-naturedly.

Palmer sent her a scornful glance. "I've got an image to consider. I can't be seen twice in the same outfit."

"Heaven forbid," Amy teased. "Which bunk do you want, top or bottom?"

"Neither one. I'm taking the single by the window," Palmer informed her.

"Let's wait until the other girls get here. Drawing numbers is the only fair way to decide who gets which bed," I said.

"Right—we've got to make sure everyone's satisfied. The four of us are used to each other, but since we'll be living with three extra people, we'll have to be extra careful not to step on each other's toes," Maxie said.

Palmer dismissed the warning with a wave of her hand. "No problem, I can get along with anybody. I didn't pay much attention to the assignment sheet. Who's in here besides us?"

"Renee Quick, for one," I answered.

"She's all right. Analyzes things to death, but she has a great sense of humor," Palmer said. "Who else?"

"Reid Olivier." Amy's nose wrinkled in distaste.

The space between Maxie's eyebrows creased into a scowl, and I wasn't exactly thrilled, either. My mom always said if I tried hard enough, I could find something to like in everyone. But for the life of me I couldn't dredge up anything positive about Reid Olivier. She was an A-one snob who always tried to impress people with how sophisticated she was. She spent money like she had a key to Fort Knox, and she was a world-class name dropper. In short, she was totally obnoxious.

"Reid is a pain sometimes," Palmer admitted. "But since her best friend, Germaine Richards, isn't around, maybe she'll be okay. Who's our seventh cabin mate?"

Amy telegraphed Maxie a worried look and Max passed it along to me. Since I was clearly elected, I cleared my throat hesitantly. But before I could break the news, the door swung open and a small figure struggled in with three bulky bags.

"Greetings, roomies," Georgette Durand chirped, depositing her load on the single cot beside the window.

Palmer's expression zipped through surprise, dismay, and irritation before it finally settled into grumpy. "I might have known," she sighed, scanning her stepsister's belongings through narrowed eyes. "You shouldn't have brought all that junk. We're very short on storage space."

"You wouldn't want me to wear the same outfit twice, would you?" Georgette asked.

Maxie nearly choked on a laugh, and I had to work hard to keep a straight face. The Durand sisters had a lot in common, although neither of them saw it that way. The

5

past year had been a constant running battle between them, and there was no reason to believe that being in the White Mountains would change that. There was no telling what the next three weeks might bring, but for sure, it wouldn't be boring.

"Knock-knock," a voice interrupted from the doorway.

A blast of heavy perfume—triple strength Jungle Musk—hit the room just before Reid Olivier. I took a step backward, breathing through my mouth to avoid the smell. Amy and Maxie obviously weren't happy campers either.

Surprisingly, Palmer was the diplomat. "How's it going, Reid? Isn't Camp Emerald the best?"

"If you're into bugs and sunstroke," Reid answered, drawing her lips into a passion-purple pout. She dumped her designer suitcase and walked over to poke at the top of the nearest cot. "This mattress is too hard, and I have to have another pillow."

"Personally, I never sleep with one—it interferes with the natural alignment of one's spine," Georgette piped up.

"Thank you for sharing that, Dr. Durand," Palmer said sarcastically. Dismissing her sister, she turned back to Reid. "Is this a great cabin, or what?"

"I suppose it beats living in a tent. But with seven people, we'll be scrunched up like sardines," Reid answered.

Oh, this is something to look forward to, I thought. *Three weeks of listening to Reid Olivier complain.* I grabbed a pen and a yellow pad from my bag and headed for the door mumbling, "I'm going down by the lake to answer Mars's letter."

Although the sun blazed directly overhead, the air was crisp and sweet. I took a huge gulp to clear the remains of

Reid's killer cologne from my lungs and started down a path that led to the woods.

Maggie Grayson-Griffith, Alma's French teacher, waved, then hurried to fall into step beside me—not easy, considering that she was about seven months pregnant. "How do you like Camp Emerald so far, Shanon?" she asked.

"It's terrific—I think."

"You'll love it when you get settled in," she assured me.

I stole a sidewise peek at her ballooning stomach. I always feel so rude when I look at a pregnant woman's stomach, but I can't help it. I've always got a million questions. I decided to start with a soft one: "Have you and Mr. G. picked out a name for the baby, yet?"

"Aloysius for a boy, and Hermione for a girl."

I nearly said, "Oh, please!" and then I realized Maggie was teasing. "How about Gustave Griswold Griffith or Gertrude Geranium Griffith?" I suggested. "Either way you could nickname it Gee-Gee-Gee."

Maggie chuckled. "Dan and I have worn out our name-your-baby book, and we still haven't been able to come up with anything we both like."

A light bulb clicked on in my head. "We could have a contest while we're here at camp. You wouldn't actually have to use the winning names, but it might be fun."

"That's a terrific idea, Shanon—I'm going to tell Dan about it this very minute," she said, ruffling my hair. She headed off, her walk slow and awkward, then paused to call back, "Come by our cabin tomorrow and help me make some posters."

"Sure thing," I promised.

The Foxes of 3-D had been part of Maggie and Dan's romance from the very beginning. We'd seen them date and fall in love. We'd cried at their wedding, and now we were going to help choose a name for their first little Griffith. It was better than a soap opera!

As I turned back toward the woods, it suddenly hit me that Maggie didn't seem to mind that she'd temporarily lost her drop-dead gorgeous figure. And when she was with Dan, she positively glowed with happiness.

Is that what love was all about? I asked myself. Mars and I had had some ups and downs lately, but we were still together. And when I thought about him, I felt all fuzzy and pink inside. I also had a hard time remembering what day it was. Either I really cared for him, or I was coming down with some dread disease. Plopping down at the base of an old oak, I stared up through the leaves for a minute, then flipped open the pad and began to write.

Dear Mars,

Camp Emerald is one of the most beautiful places I've ever seen. We're down in a valley, and the White Mountains around us stretch up so high they seem to be holding up the clouds. The water in the lake is dark blue, almost navy, and the wind blows the tops of the waves into a lacy white foam. Plus, the food is scrumptious because Mrs. Butter, Alma's four-star cook, is on the job! This would be heaven—if you were here.

Besides looking at the stunning scenery, there are loads of fun things to do here—canoeing, tennis, crafts, and archery, for starters. Amy plans to spend a lot of her time on the softball field, partly because she's a super athlete, and partly because Nikos Smith is sure to be the captain of one of the teams. I hope Maxie and Paul Grant smooth things out. They're still ridiculously shy if they're within a mile of another human being. Palmer is Palmer—what else can I say? I expected her to blow a gasket when she found out that Georgette is one of our cabin mates, but she handled it pretty well.

Speaking of cabin mates, Renee Quick is our number six. I met her last term, I thing she's pretty cool all-around. She's smart and confident and likes drama. She wrote and helped produce the third-form play. Her folks have money, but she doesn't seem spoiled. All in all, I think she'll work out fine.

It's a safe bet that Reid Olivier (number seven) is going to be big trouble. There aren't too many people who rub me the wrong way, but she's one of them. Amy and Maxie aren't wild about her, either. And I know she used to really get on Palmer's nerves, but now Palmer actually seems to like her. Who can figure Palmer?

Now for the bad news about the next three weeks. Besides missing you, I'm going to have to take the swimming test I failed last year. I don't have to tell you that I absolutely, positively hate *water that's not in a bathtub*, and I'm scared stiff every time I get near it. Even worse, there will be a "survival" weekend at the end of camp. I heard that Mr. Griffith's setting up special exercises—like finding the way out of a spooky cave, and jumping from a tall pole to a trapeze that's nine feet away. Sounds like fun, huh? Let's just say that I am totally terrified.

But knowing that I'm your best girl is going to help get me through it all in one piece. Every time I'm tempted to wimp out, I'll remember that I want you to be proud of me.

You must be really depressed about missing out on this vacation, but I'll write often and keep you filled in. If you still have on your cast next time I see you, I'll sign it:

All my love,
Shanon

TIME CAPSULE
ENTRY TWO:
BY MAXIE SCHLOSS

———————◆———————

Dear Maxie,

Last time you wrote, you asked for more information about me. You might fall asleep while you're reading this letter, because my story isn't exactly a page-turner. As I've told you before, I'm just an average 5'9" guy with a cowlick and green eyes.

Although in real years I'm fourteen, I've only had three birthdays because I was born on February 29. The years when the calendar skips over me, I get presents on March 1, but every Leap Year, my mom makes a four-layer coconut cake (my favorite), four gallons of homemade peach ice cream (ditto), and I get to invite all the people I like most to a party. The next bash won't be until I'm sixteen, but consider this your advance invitation!

The main events in my life are water sports—sailing, scuba, skin diving, and wind surfing. I learned to swim when I was six months old, and I'm a lot happier wet than dry. I suppose that's not surprising for a Pisces.

What else can I tell you? I love science fiction (particularly anything written by Isaac Asimov) and I hate brussels sprouts. That about sums up the life and times of Paul M. Grant. By the way, don't bother asking what my middle initial stands for—that's one secret I'm taking with me to the great beyond!

Regards,
Paul

I had read the old letter my pen pal sent during the school year so many times that the paper was beginning to shred. What I was looking for was the key to Paul Grant's personality, some clue that would tell me what went on under that golden blond hair. What I got was mostly vital statistics. If I really stretched the point, the invitation to his next birthday party meant that I was one of his favorite people. Other than that, the letter was about as romantic as one I'd write to my great-aunt Sophie.

On the up side—besides us both being nearly the same height and having green eyes—it was amazing how much Paul and I had in common: I loved water so much that I should have been born with scales, and sci-fi was my absolute passion.

Refolding the letter into a small square, I stuck it in my pocket and glanced around the cabin. There were enough clothes scattered around the far side to open a boutique. Which was not surprising since Palmer, Georgette, and Reid had drawn the winning numbers for the single beds. Halfway through unpacking, the trio had gone off to raid coat hangers from the other girls' cabins.

Shanon and I were lucky to be sharing the bunk bed diagonally across from Reid's cot. My nose needed as much distance as possible from the Olivier "eau de bug spray" perfume.

"I'm on my way to the field to see if the sign-up sheets for the teams have been posted. Want to come, Maxie?" Amy asked, slicking gloss over her lips. She had changed outfits four times in the last three minutes, which meant that she was as interested in finding Nikos Smith as in being first on the softball roster.

"I'll catch up with you for lunch in the mess hall," I said, not wanting to interfere if she did find Nikos. "Right now I think I'll go check out the pool."

Amy's mouth eased into a teasing grin. "Looking for anyone in particular, or will any old Pisces named Paul do?"

"Never mind," I said quickly. Don't ask me why, but I have a hard time talking about Paul. Maybe it's because everything is still so new between us that I'm never really sure of where I stand.

Amy swept the length of her straight black hair into a ponytail, eyeing me curiously. "Have you told Paul you're crazy about him?"

"Of course not!" I changed the subject: "How did you really feel about your ex–pen pal, John Adams?"

She frowned as though trying to find just the right answer. "It was fun writing songs with him, and we got to be good friends. The relationship wasn't going anywhere, though—there wasn't any big charge when we were together. Know what I mean?"

I didn't, but I nodded anyway.

Amy propped her elbows on the dresser, then rested her chin on her hands. "Nikos is really different. We've gotten to be really good friends, but we haven't talked about

13

anything serious—yet. I hope we'll get around to it while we're here."

I decided to ask the question I'd been trying to answer since the first time I saw Paul Grant. "Amy, how do you know when you're in love?"

"Beats me. Maybe we should ask Palmer—she takes the plunge at least once a week," Amy joked. "Walk me as far as the mess hall, then we'll split up. I think we could both use a little moral support."

"Okay, but I'd better change first." I got up to rummage through the clothes I'd just stashed in the chest beside my bed. Before I left New York, I'd gone to Bloomie's and blown my life's savings on a shorts set that I thought might impress Paul. Holding the outfit in front of me, I wasn't so sure. "What do you think?" I asked.

"It's great"—she took a deep breath, then pressed on—"for Palmer. Sorry, but preppy isn't your style, Max. You'd do better to go with your own look."

Which at the moment was an oversize Hard Rock Café T-shirt, baggy denims whacked off above the knees, mismatched socks, and high-top running shoes. Since I was totally comfortable just the way I was, I decided that Amy had a good point. Picking up my hat—a Bullwinkle baseball cap with padded felt antlers sticking out from the sides—I settled it on my red hair. "Okay, pal, let's go hunting!"

The quadrangle that divided the boys' cabins from the girls' was jammed with campers from both sides. The upper-form kids generally paired off into couples. In the lower forms, the boys hung out with the boys, and the girls hung out with the girls. Not too long ago, I would have been solidly in the second group. But now, I was caught some-

14

where in the middle: Part of me wanted to run back to the good old days, the rest voted to be with Paul. Whoever invented hormones definitely had a warped sense of humor.

"There's Renee Quick," Amy said, pointing to the model-skinny, very pretty girl getting out of a limo parked in the gravel driveway. Amy headed away from me with a cheery, "I'll run over and tell her that she's sharing my bunk."

I was about to follow when Palmer jogged up beside me and grabbed my arm. "I was supposed to meet Reid here so we could go to lunch together. Have you seen her?" she asked.

"Nope, so far I've been lucky. Palmer, are you sure you want to get involved with her? Reid's a real weirdo, and we both know how sneaky she can be. Remember the dirty trick she and Germaine pulled on you?"

"Reid says she had nothing to do with it," Palmer said defensively. "Anyway, I don't need your advice on how to pick my friends."

I knew why she was so mad, and it didn't have anything to do with Reid. Things had gotten pretty tense between us at the end of the school term when she'd tried to steal Paul from me. Like a lot of Palmer's schemes, it didn't work. I figured now was a good time to bury the hatchet. "I'd really like for us to get along while we're here at camp, Palmer. If you're still ticked off because of Paul—"

"No hard feelings. I'd completely forgotten about it until you brought it up," she cut me off with a nonchalant shrug. "And anyway, I was never really interested in Paul Grant. Your cousin, Rain, is so much more mature and exciting. As a matter of fact, I just sent him a long letter."

15

"Really?" I said. "The last I heard, Rain was headed for Europe with his parents. Aunt Claudia and Uncle Frank hate schedules, so we never know where they're liable to turn up. Did Rain decide to stay home?"

"Well, er—" Palmer licked her lips as though they'd suddenly gone dry, then her face brightened. "No, but we still write each other. His mail goes to a credit card company, and they deliver it."

"That's neat." It sounded a little fishy to me, but I let it go and took another stab at a truce. "What I said about Reid Olivier might've been a little out of line. It's just that I don't trust her, and I'd hate to see you get hurt."

"Thanks," she said, her expression softening. "I'm glad we're friends again. Guys aren't worth arguing over. Besides, I'm not really into boys at the moment—at least, none of the ones at Emerald Lake," she confided. "I'm going to concentrate on improving my tennis game while I'm here."

I tried not to look shocked, but it was almost as if she'd announced that she'd decided to shave her head! The two main events in Palmer's life were clothes and boys—not necessarily in that order.

Before I could ask what caused her change of heart, she glanced past me and waved frantically. "There's Reid now," she announced, hurrying away.

I turned back to the path that led to the pool. I was almost there when I spotted a guy with sun-streaked hair in the crowd. His back was to me, but he was about the right height and weight. Fighting off an insane urge to head in the opposite direction, I pushed my way through the pack and tapped him on the shoulder. He turned—dimpled, golden blond, and gorgeous.

16

But he wasn't Paul.

I thought I would die of embarrassment. Mumbling the lame excuse that I'd mistaken him for my brother, I set a world's record for retreat. I didn't stop running until I was through the grove of trees that ringed the camp and on the shore of the lake.

Furious at myself for being such a dweeb, I picked up a stick and started gouging holes in the moist sand. When I realized that I might've had the same reaction if the blond stranger *had* been Paul, I got even madder. For fourteen years, I, Maxine Edith Schloss, had been a happy-go-lucky, boy-hating klutz. Then Paul Grant came along and zap—I turned into a moony-eyed, rubber-kneed, tongue-tied klutz. The worst part was that I couldn't be sure how Paul felt about me. His letters were great, and the few times we'd been alone together had been better than excellent. But when other people were around, we both clammed up. Who needed that kind of hassle?

Obviously, I did, because while my brain was fighting it, my hand had drawn a lopsided heart in the sand. In its center were the initials M.E.S. and P.M.G.

"That is amazing headgear," Paul's voice said from behind.

For once, I had lightning-quick reflexes; I scrambled to my feet and scuffed away the drawing in the same motion. "Hi," I said. "Bet you never thought you'd meet Bullwinkle in the White Mountains."

Grinning, Paul tweaked one of my felt antlers. "Weirder things have happened."

Yeah, I thought, *like me meeting you.* Paul was wearing crisp navy tennis shorts that matched his socks and a snug-fitting pullover. When I focused on the tiny alligator embroidered on the pocket of his shirt, Amy's words came back loud and clear: "Preppy isn't your style, Max."

The clothes that had been so right on me when I left the cabin now felt like a clown costume. To fill the silence that was stretching between us, I did what I'd done since I was three years old—I launched into a comic routine. "Emerald Lake reminds me of that old joke about the three campers who . . ." The smile that tugged at his mouth made me forget the punchline, so I swallowed hard and asked, "Why am I babbling?"

"For the same reason I'm standing here like a zombie with amnesia. I guess we're both a little uptight."

Summoning my courage, I lifted my head to meet his gaze. "If we weren't, what do you suppose we'd be talking about?"

"Which activities we're going to sign up for together." He took a deep breath and added, "And how glad we are to see each other."

"For sure." It was hard for me to keep from turning a cartwheel on the spot, but I managed. "What about senior lifesaving, kayaking, and springboard diving?"

"You must be reading my mind!" His smile widened and he reached to tuck a stray strand of my hair behind my ear.

This was a moment I'd remember all my life—the clean, soft smell of the wind, the sound of waves kissing the sandy shore, and most of all, the steady warmth in Paul Grant's green eyes.

TIME CAPSULE
ENTRY THREE:
BY PALMER DURAND

———————◦———————

My dearest, darling Rain,

I can't imagine why I thought it would be fun to come to the Alma/Ardsley summer outdoor program—it's like getting dumped into a U.S. Marine boot camp! At five-thirty this morning, I was dreaming of you when a siren started to howl. I thought we were being attacked by terrorists, but it was only the wake-up signal. Then Kate Majors marched into our cabin and started barking orders. I had to make my bed twice before it passed inspection!

Even worse than that, my stepsister, Georgette, has the cot right next to mine! I'd much rather have shared a double-decker with Amy—that way, it would have been like we were still in Suite 3-D—but Shanon (who's got this complex about being fair) insisted that we draw numbers for our spaces.

Reid Olivier is on the other side of me. The rest of the girls in our cabin dump on her, but now that she's away from her creepy best friend, Germaine, she isn't so bad. The only problem I see is that she wears awful perfume.

I haven't spent much time with my suitemates lately.

Shanon is wrapped up in a video project, and Maxine spends all her time in the water with Paul Grant. I thought it might be neat if Amy and I signed up for archery together, but she's too busy chasing Nikos Smith.

My main problem is that you're so far away. I always kiss your picture before I go to sleep. Then I dream of the magic day when you'll hold me in your strong arms and tell me I'm the most wonderful woman in the universe.

Passionately yours,
Palmer Durand

Even as I signed my name and licked the flap of the envelope, I was having second thoughts about the letter I'd just written. Most of it seemed kind of whiny, and the last paragraph—which I'd copied from a paperback—came on too strong. Not that it mattered much: Rain would never read it because I had no idea where to send it. In fact, until Maxie broke the news, I hadn't even known that he was going to Europe. I'd met him once—at Maxie's Christmas party last year—and we'd only written each other a couple of times since. I hated to admit it, even to myself, but my romance with Rain Blackburn was mostly in my head.

I stared at the blank face of the envelope for a long minute, then ripped up the letter. "Boys are so boring," I muttered to myself.

"Were you talking to me?" Georgette, the only other person in the cabin, stopped rummaging in her duffel bag to stare at me.

"I just decided to give up guys forever," I announced.

"That's nice." Her blank smile told me she wasn't really

paying attention. "Have you seen the binoculars Dad sent me yesterday? I'm going bird-watching with Renee, and I can't find them anywhere."

I couldn't believe that *my* father had given her another present. The whole two days I'd been at Emerald Lake, I'd only gotten a postcard from him.

"Their focus is quite remarkable," Georgette added in her "Little Miss Encyclopedia" voice. "Renee says her father has a pair like them. He's an attorney, you know, and her mother—"

"—is a caterer. You've only mentioned that a thousand times," I snapped, beginning to get really irritated.

I didn't have anything against Renee—in fact, I kind of liked her. But lately, her name started and ended every sentence that came out of Georgette's mouth.

"Here they are," Georgette said, pulling the binoculars from her bag. She slung the strap of the leather case over her shoulder and trotted away without so much as a good-bye.

I don't get it. I spent most of my time this past year figuring out ways to avoid the brat. So why was I bent out of shape because she left me alone?

Maybe you're jealous of her new friendship with Renee, a voice inside my head whispered.

"I couldn't care less who the pest hangs out with," I answered aloud.

Arguing with my conscience wasn't something I did very often, and I wasn't thrilled that the other me had scored a point. Feeling totally depressed, I got up and wandered outside.

My plans for a life without boys were canceled when I saw Nikos Smith coming toward me. Nikos is a super jock. Needless to say, he's very well built. Plus he's got this gorgeous dark hair. "Hi, Nikos," I said.

"Hello, Palmer." He didn't even look at me. "Amy and I are due at batting practice. Is she around?"

"She left fifteen minutes ago," I told him.

He spun on his heel with a short, "See you around."

Things hadn't been going well for me lately—I'd lost both Sam O'Leary and Paul Grant. And it was plain to see that Nikos wasn't interested. If I hadn't known better, I'd have thought the great Palmer Durand was losing her touch.

"Are you thinking of starting a thing with macho-man Smith?" Reid asked, coming up from behind.

"That would be totally sneaky!" I protested. "Even though the creep did come on to me, he's still Amy's pen pal." The lie popped out before I could stop it. Even though I felt guilty, it gave me back a little of my self-confidence.

"That's the price you pay for looking so good," Reid said philosophically. "You have to put up with so much junk." She sighed and handed me a plastic garbage bag.

"What's this for?"

"Trash. We've been assigned to clear up half the quadrangle," she informed me glumly. "Camp rules say everybody has to do chores. It's supposed to be good for morale."

"As much as my father paid out to get me into this backwoods hole, you'd think they could afford to hire janitors," I grumbled, trailing along beside her.

"Before we start cleanup duty, let's check out what's happening," she said, leading the way to the bulletin board by the mailbox.

I wasn't interested in the classes that were posted, but

the camp roster caught my eye: The names of the Ardies were listed by class. Though I knew most of the younger guys, the seniors were new territory. "Kevin Ashford, Drake DeWitt," I read aloud. "On a scale of one to ten, those names rate about a seven."

"How about Curtis Custis?" Reid asked.

"Minus two. I'll bet he likes hillbilly music and picks his teeth with a straw."

She giggled. "Perfect!"

I grinned at the compliment and moved a fingernail down the list. "Holbrook Wellington is a definite ten. I'd say he's going to an Ivy League college after he graduates." My imagination supplied a detailed picture of a dark-haired hunk with violet eyes. He was stepping out of a Porsche convertible.

"If you two don't want a bunch of demerits, you'd better get cracking on the cleanup detail. This area will be inspected before lunch," Kate Majors informed us on her way past.

"She's always on my case," Reid muttered, glaring at the upper-former's back.

Though our dorm monitor could get on my nerves, she had a lot of good points. But it wouldn't have been cool to defend her, so I kept my mouth shut.

The sun was blazing hot, and picking up soda cans and apple cores gave me the creeps. I didn't like to clean up my own mess, much less someone else's. I was stooping over for a scrap of paper when I got the feeling that someone was watching me. As I straightened up, I saw a short, pasty-faced guy standing nearby. His thick, wire-rimmed glasses and dweeby deck shoes practically screamed the word "NERD."

"H-hello," he stammered, looking at me adoringly.

A few days ago, I would've ignored him. But with nothing better to do, I turned on the Durand charm and answered, "Hi, there."

He went into immediate meltdown.

Giggling, Reid whispered, "You'd better ditch your geeky boyfriend. We've only got fifteen minutes to finish."

I sighed and dragged myself toward a candy wrapper that was lying on the grass.

Nerdo beat me to it. "You might get dirty. I'll get it," he offered.

"Thanks a lot." I gave him a knock-'em-dead smile.

"While you're at it, you can do mine, too," Reid ordered, handing him her plastic bag. Linking arms with me, she pointed to a clump of trees across the driveway. "Let's go over there where we can talk in private."

We were ten yards away from the kid before I realized I hadn't even asked his name

"So, are you going after Holbrook Wellington?" Reid asked when we settled in the shade of an elm.

"I doubt it." I yanked up a daisy and began shredding its petals, finishing, "Boys are such duds."

"You can say that again. But as long as we're stuck here, it might be neat to have an Ardie boyfriend. Don't you think Rob Williams is kind of cute?"

"He's not my type. Besides, he and Lisa McGreevy have a thing going. Even though she left Alma, she's still one of the Foxes, so it wouldn't be cool for me to move in on Rob."

Reid smiled. "You're too loyal, but I can respect that. Still, since you know him so well, would you introduce him to me?"

24

"It wouldn't do you much good. He and Lisa are pretty tight—they write each other all the time," I told her, hoping she'd drop the subject.

No such luck. "But Lisa's not here, and I'm sure Rob is lonesome," Reid went on. "It wouldn't hurt anyone if I just kept him company."

I was out of arguments, so I finally agreed. "I wouldn't mention this to Shanon, though. She's Lisa's closest friend and she'll get hyper if she thinks you're trying to snatch Rob."

"That's because she's so juvenile. Really, Palmer, you ought to take pity on that girl and teach her a thing or two." Reid unzipped the jogger's pouch she wore strapped around her waist and retrieved a pack of cigarettes. "Want one?"

I shook my head, trying not to look shocked.

Reid lit up and started to cough. "I've only been doing this for a couple of weeks, and I'm not very good at it yet," she confessed. "How long have you been smoking?"

"Ages," I lied. "I decided to quit while I'm here, though. My nosy stepsister is always borrowing my clothes, and if she smelled smoke on them, she'd be sure to tell my dad."

"After you're through, you can spray yourself with some of my perfume. It covers up anything." Reid tossed the pack and a book of matches into my lap. "It's more fun if both of us do it."

The thought of my clothes reeking with smoke and Jungle Musk (which Amy had already renamed Jungle Muck) was not exactly appealing. But the expectant expression on Reid's face backed me into a corner: If I didn't light up, she'd think I was a goody-goody.

"Okay—why not?"

My first drag answered the question: My chest felt as though it had been stabbed with an ice pick, and there was a sharp, nasty taste in my mouth. I plopped down on the ground choking and hacking. "What's in these things?" I wheezed.

"Menthol. It's supposed to be good for your sinuses."

"No wonder I'm coughing. I only smoke the plain ones," I sputtered. Before I could pull myself together, a crunching sound came from a nearby clump of bushes: Someone was coming! I scrambled to my feet and Reid's face went chalky white.

She quickly ground the butt into the dirt, snapping out a panicked, "Who's there?"

"Me." The foliage parted and the nerd shuffled up.

"Why were you spying on us?" I demanded, glaring at him.

"I wasn't spying. I just came to tell you I finished the cleaning detail." His dishwater gray eyes were seriously troubled as he added, "Smoking is very bad for you."

"Where do you get off telling us what to do?" Reid's eyes narrowed to slits, and she growled, "If you say one word about this, you're dog food."

He backed away from her. "I wouldn't do anything to get Palmer into trouble."

"How do you know who I am?" I asked, startled.

"The guys at school talk about you all the time. Everyone says you're the most beautiful girl at Alma Stephens."

The explanation went a long way toward making his company acceptable. "What's your name?" I asked.

"Holbrook Wellington."

So much for my fantasy about the hunk in the Porsche.

26

Reid let out a hoot. "Get real! Holbrook Wellington is a senior—you can't be any older than fourteen."

"I'm thirteen, and I'm graduating next year because I'm in the gifted students program." He gave me a pleading look, switching to, "I know you have pen pals at Ardsley. Will you write to me, too, Palmer?"

I was pretty sure he wouldn't rat on me for smoking, but I wasn't taking any chances. "Maybe. I like people who know how to keep their mouths shut," I said, smiling. "Are you from Massachusetts?"

He shook his head solemnly. "New Jersey. Why do you ask?"

"I thought you might be related to the Boston Wellingtons."

"You mean the millionaires? I wish I were—then maybe my father wouldn't have to drive a cab." Holbrook peeked at his watch, then shot a worried look back toward the quadrangle. "If we don't hurry, we're going to miss lunch. It would be great if the two of you sat with me."

Although I couldn't be positive, I thought I heard a hint of blackmail in his tone. I decided that sharing a table with a penniless, brainy nerd would be a lot worse than getting demerits for breaking the no-smoking rule.

Before I could refuse the invitation, Reid cut in, "We've got a few things to do first. You go ahead and save seats for us."

He nodded happily and skittered away.

"Have you lost your mind? Our reputations will be ruined if we're seen with that geek!" I snapped at her when Holbrook was out of earshot.

"We're not going to have lunch with him. I just said that to get rid of him."

"If we don't show up, he might tell on us," I warned.

"Next time we see him, we'll say we couldn't make it because one of the counselors gave us more chores to do."

"Then he'll invite us again and we'll have to make up another lie—it could go on for the whole three weeks," I sighed.

"That's just what I had in mind." Reid lit another cigarette, blowing smoke from her lungs in a long plume. "If we play our cards right, we won't have to do any more chores. All you have to do is bat your eyes at him and he'll be our slave for the rest of the time we're here."

The plan was brilliant, but if Amy, Maxie, and Shanon suspected I was flirting with Holbrook to avoid chores, I'd never hear the end of it. Ditto for the cigarettes, I thought, cringing at the possibility that Georgette might pick up their smell on me. Without a doubt, she would break her neck getting to the phone to call Dad.

"Hurry up and finish so we can split," I told Reid, moving upwind of the cloud around her. "I need to go shampoo my hair."

TIME CAPSULE
ENTRY FOUR:
BY AMY HO

Dear Amy,

You might think it's weird that I'm writing you a letter when I can talk to you face-to-face. But I thought you might like a description of your outstanding performance on the softball field for the Foxes' time capsule! The way you snagged that pop-up today during practice drills was really excellent, and Coach Barker told me your E.R.A. was out of sight. You've got one of the greatest arms I've ever seen on a girl!

By the way, I've got something very important to ask you. Meet me outside the mess hall this afternoon at five.

Nikos

P.S. Hope my "sports-speak" doesn't confuse you. E.R.A. means "Earned Run Average," not "Equal Rights Amendment."

I was tired, hot, and thirsty after softball practice, and for some reason, the ending of the note I'd found tucked in my mitt rubbed me the wrong way. "I know just as much about softball as Nikos Smith. That P.S. sounds like a put-down to me," I told Shanon irritably as we tacked a poster for the "name-the-Griffith-baby" contest on a tree near the boys' cabins.

"I'm sure he was only teasing," she answered.

"You're probably right," I agreed. "I wish we were playing for the same team during the tournament."

"I thought you were."

"He's the captain of the Avengers and I got picked to be on the Ninja Turtles," I explained. "I wonder what he wants to talk to me about?"

"I'll bet he's going to ask you to go out with him," Shanon predicted.

"That would be too"—I couldn't find a word special enough to describe my feelings, so I settled for—"rad."

"To say the least. It means that you'll be dating a V.I.P. Ardie—Mars says Nikos is sure to be the quarterback of the football team next year."

My instant vision was of Nikos fading back to arch a perfect strike into the end zone, and then after winning the game, sweeping me into his arms. The fantasy was so real that I nearly forgot to breathe. "He's a terrific athlete, but there's much more to him than muscles," I sighed, hugging my arms tight across my chest. "He always seems so sure of himself. Like he never has any doubts or fears."

Shanon giggled. "I never thought I'd live to see the day Amy Ho would go bonkers about a guy!"

"Me, either," I admitted, squirming, "and it's kind of hard getting used to it. I never felt anything like this when John and I were together."

30

"Shhhhh!" Shanon poked me in the ribs, her eyes focused on a spot off to my left.

When I followed the line of her gaze, I saw the subject of my last sentence coming down the path. Hoping that he hadn't overheard, I pasted on a guilty smile and waved.

"Hey, John—check out the poster I helped Maggie make," Shanon chattered as he walked up to us.

"Nice," he said without much enthusiasm.

"Are you going to enter the baby-naming contest?" I asked.

He avoided my gaze. "I doubt it."

His coldness stung a little, but it didn't really surprise me. From the minute we'd set foot in camp, he'd been ignoring me. We had been close once, though, and even if we were no longer pen pals, I didn't see any reason why we couldn't still be friends.

"First prize is a week's supply of pizza from Figaro's," I pointed out. "As creative as you are, I'll bet you could come up with a great set of names."

"That kind of stuff is strictly for girls," he sneered, stalking off.

"I wonder what his problem is," I muttered.

"I think he's still hurt because you dumped him this year," Shanon said gently.

"I'm glad I did. I don't like guys who make male chauvinist cracks!"

"You don't have time to get bent out of shape about it now. It's a quarter to five," she said, checking her watch.

"Yikes! I can't meet Nikos looking like this!" My hands flew immediately to my hair, at the moment a bunch of limp strands straggling around my face. "I need to wash my hair, my nails are an absolute mess, and—"

31

"—you've got a big smudge of dirt on your nose," Shanon finished, fishing tissue, a comb, and a lipstick from her hip pack. "Lucky for you I came prepared for any emergency."

"A tune-up won't cut it—I need a major overhaul," I said, turning to dash toward the cabin.

For the next twenty minutes I went through a complete makeover, snagging a shower and fresh clothes on the run. While Maxie zapped my hair with a blow dryer, Shanon threw makeup in the general direction of my face.

At the same time, Palmer kept up a running stream of tips on how to handle boys—most of which I promptly forgot the minute I stepped out of the door.

As promised in the note, Nikos was waiting for me in front of the mess hall.

"Sorry I'm late," I apologized breathlessly as I jogged up to his side at 5:08.

"No problem, I know how long it takes you all to do things," he said with a grin.

"You all?" I echoed, not quite catching the drift of his comment.

Instead of clearing up my confusion, he said, "It was worth the wait—you look great."

My "Thanks" came out somewhere between a squeak and a croak.

"I pigged out at lunch today, so I'm not very hungry. Are you?"

Although I could have eaten an elephant with a side order of hippopotamus, I shook my head.

"Good. Let's skip dinner and go for a walk," he suggested, draping one arm casually around my shoulders.

If it hadn't been for the weight of his hand, I think I

would've floated away. His touch did other weird things to me, too. My mouth was cotton-dry and all I could remember of Palmer's advice was to ask Nikos questions about himself. It was a minor miracle that I managed to blurt out, "Do you like rap music?"

"It's okay." Nikos slid me a glance from under his lashes. "I heard that you and John used to write songs together."

"We did a couple of things," I mumbled, feeling heat beginning to rise in my cheeks. This surely wasn't the direction I'd planned for the conversation to take, but I couldn't think of another subject to switch to, so I pressed on, "Rap is okay, but I really prefer heavy metal, don't you?"

"I don't know very much about music." He steered me off the path, and settling on a grassy, sunlit spot, he pulled me down beside him, adding, "It would blow my mom away if I learned to play the guitar, though—she's always wanted at least one of her five sons to do something musical. Do you think you could teach me?"

"I'd be glad to! We can start tomorrow after practice," I told him. From the way his expression softened when he mentioned his mother, it was easy to tell she was pretty special to him. "Is your mom a musician?"

"She was a ballerina before she married my dad. She still teaches a few classes, but mostly she just takes care of the house."

Giving up a ballet career to do laundry and dishes didn't seem like a smart move to me, but I wasn't about to say so. I just said, "Ballet dancers are really good athletes."

"That's for sure! My mom plays a mean game of softball," Nikos said proudly. "You know, you remind me a lot of her. Both of you have terrific coordination."

His smile told me I'd just been paid the ultimate compliment. "Thanks—that's very nice to hear," I said, blushing. Then I got up my courage and asked, "Was that what you wanted to talk to me about?"

His arm slid away from my shoulder, and he clasped his hands around his knees. "That and my softball team. I want you to be my starting pitcher for the tournament next week."

I looked at him as if he'd just asked me to fly to the moon with him. "I thought the lineups were already set," I said.

He plucked a long blade of grass and nibbled the end of it absently as he explained, "They were, but this afternoon I talked with Phyllis McGill, the captain of the Turtles. She's willing to trade you to the Avengers if I give her Bill Lundy and John Adams."

"Two for one?" I squealed, stunned beyond belief.

He frowned. "Actually, it's an even trade. I've got to take Renee Quick, too."

Even at that, it was still pretty incredible that he'd let Bill and John go just to get me. They were the Avengers' best hitters, and my batting average was only decent at best. "I don't get it—you're the Avengers' pitcher. Why would you bench yourself and start me?"

"I twisted my elbow while I was sliding into second. It's not bad, but I won't be ready to go back on the mound for at least another week," he answered, grimacing. "The Avengers need you, Amy, and so do I. Will you do it?"

It took a lot of control to keep my "Yes" from turning into a whoop of joy. "I'll tell Phyllis tonight."

"That's okay. I was pretty sure you'd agree, so I already went ahead with the trade."

It suddenly struck me wrong that he'd swapped me without asking first—as though I were a baseball card or a comic book instead of a person. And just as quickly, it occurred to me that the deal between Nikos and Phyllis could have been the reason for John's snit earlier that afternoon. Given his new macho attitude, my ex–pen pal probably wasn't thrilled to be playing for a female softball captain!

"Is something wrong? You've got the strangest look on your face," Nikos observed, frowning.

"I guess I'm kind of nervous," I lied. "I don't want to let you down."

"You could never do that." Taking a Snickers bar from his shirt pocket, he peeled off the wrapper and shared the candy with me. "I like being with you, Amy. You're a good sport, and you know more about baseball than most girls."

"Most boys, too," I said between bites. A faint alarm went off in my head, but I ignored it. "What do you think of the New York Mets this year?"

"All flash and no heart. The Chicago Cubs are the best team in the National League East," Nikos answered.

I snorted. "In your dreams. The Cubbies always fade in the stretch. They're already twelve games out of first place, and . . ." I trailed off, stopped by the rock-hard set of his jaw. "Wait—you can't possibly be a Cubs fan! Those turkeys have never won a World Series!"

"They have so! Back in 1908, they beat Detroit four to one."

"Yeah, and Fred Flintstone was the manager," I teased, giggling. The sparks crackling from the depths of Nikos's eyes warned me that he was getting mad, but I couldn't stop while I was on a roll. "That was so long ago that the sports page was carved on stone tablets!"

There's no telling where the argument would have gone if John Adams hadn't come hurrying along the path. "I've been looking all over for you, Nikos. The guys in Cabin Five want us to shoot some hoops with them," he said, his words and tone making it clear that I wasn't included.

"Nikos has a sore arm," I said coolly.

"Yeah, but a little exercise might work out some of the kinks." Nikos got up and stretched, adding, "You don't mind if I split, do you, Amy?"

"No problem," I said, trying not to sound hurt because he was leaving.

As the two of them strolled away, their voices carried back to me clearly through the still air.

"You weren't actually talking baseball to Amy, were you?" John scoffed. "Girls don't know anything about sports."

"Tell me about it. She actually had the nerve to dump on the Cubs," Nikos replied.

I stared at his retreating back, confused and beginning to get angry. Could it be that Nikos Smith, the guy I was so crazy about, was a macho pig?

TIME CAPSULE
ENTRY FIVE:
BY GEORGETTE
DURAND

Dear Georgette,

Thanks for the new word you sent me. It's definitely a change to have a pen pal who likes words as much as I do. I'll be waiting for your next tongue-twister.

The Foxes' time capsule sounds like a great idea. Is Palmer as much into it as everyone else? When we were pen pals, the letters she sent me were barely a page long, so it's hard for me to imagine her writing two or three whole chapters. By the way, what's she been up to lately? Is she having fun at Camp Emerald?

Write me soon. You're a really cute kid and I enjoy your letters.

All my best,
Sam O'Leary

"Sam's still interested in Palmer," I sighed, pushing my breakfast tray aside to spread out the letter on the table. "I think he's only writing me so he can keep tabs on her."

"Maybe. But at least you're getting mail from him."
Renee Quick snitched a slice of my bacon and crunched on
it absently as she continued, "And every time you answer
one of his letters, you've got another chance to make him
forget Palmer and concentrate on you."

"Are you suggesting that I"—I paused to glance around
the nearly deserted mess hall, making sure no one was
close enough to overhear before finishing—"*sabotage* my
own stepsister?"

"Of course not! That would be dishonest and sneaky,"
Renee answered, her forehead wrinkling with disapproval.
"Maybe you need to punch up your presentation—loosen
up a little. Sam already knows that you're brainy and cute,
but you've got to make him see that you're also funny,
interesting, and creative."

"Are you trying to tell me that my letters are boring?"

"To tell the truth, they're not best-seller material. For
instance, in your last letter you told Sam that Camp Emerald 'presents a wide variety of gratifying, stimulating,
and highly enjoyable experiences.' "

"That's a perfectly accurate description," I said stiffly.

"Yeah, but it sounds like a brochure for a senior citizens'
home. Most kids our age would say 'Camp Emerald has all
sorts of fun stuff to do.' "

I was tempted to remind her that I wasn't like most kids
our age, but that would have sounded like bragging. As
much as I hated to admit it, though, Renee was probably
right. From now on, my notes to Sam would be simple and
straight to the point, I decided. "Can I at least keep the
vocabulary game going?" I asked out loud. "Sam considers
it fascina—er, I mean, he likes it a lot."

38

Renee grinned at me. "So do I. What's the next word you're going to send him?"

"Syzygy." I took out the tiny pocket dictionary I always carry, and flipped to the definition. "Syzygy," I quoted, "the nearly straight-line configuration of three heavenly bodies (as the sun, moon, and earth during a solar or lunar eclipse) in a gravitational system."

Renee's eyes widened and she let out a long whistle. "Would you break that down into something I can handle?"

"It's very simple." I spaced the salt and pepper shakers a foot apart on the table, then set the catsup bottle directly between them. "These are the heavenly bodies. When they're all lined up in a row like this, the system is called a syzygy."

"Of course," Renee teased. "It's perfectly obvious." She peeked at her watch, then scrambled to her feet. "We're going to be late for arts and crafts if we don't hurry."

"Go ahead so you can save us a space by the window. I'll be there in a few minutes." I propped my elbows on the table, and stared at the example I'd set up—and something mind-boggling occurred to me: I was part of a syzygy, with Sam at the other end of the line, and Palmer stuck dead in the middle!

I stood up, but before I picked up my tray, I moved the catsup bottle to the other side of the table. "That's much better," I said to myself, smiling as I studied the new arrangement: Georgette, the salt shaker, now had a clear shot at Sam, the pepper. Why couldn't life be that simple? Getting rid of the catsup bottle was a snap, but at the moment, I didn't have the slightest idea how to go about moving my stepsister's heavenly body out of the way.

I started toward the front of the mess hall to dump my tray, so caught up in the problem that I almost bumped into another camper.

"Watch where you're going," Palmer grumbled, side-stepping just in time to avoid a collision.

"You've already missed breakfast. You should've gotten out of bed when . . ." I trailed off, gaping at the floppy apron that was draped over her pale blue cotton jumpsuit. "Why are you dressed like that?"

"Because I'm on my way to a formal dance, dum-dum!" she shot back sarcastically. The irritation in her expression changed to gloom as she explained, "My chore for today is to clear the tables and refill the catsup bottles."

A twinge of guilt over my syzygy experiment forced patches of bright red into my cheeks. "My turn at K.P. duty was yesterday after lunch. It's not so bad," I said, eyeing Palmer with some alarm. Her shoulders sagged, her mouth was droopy, and the ribbon that held her hair in a ponytail didn't match anything she was wearing. This was definitely not the Palmer I was used to arguing with! "Is something wrong?" I asked.

"I wish I'd never come to this stupid camp! It's totally boring and all the guys are dweebs!" Palmer clamped her lips tight and marched off toward the nearest table.

Curiosity and concern made me follow. "There may be a few losers here," I admitted. "But there are drop-dead gorgeous Ardies all over the place. Why aren't you interested in any of them?"

She hesitated a long while before answering, "Because

40

none of them seem to be interested in me. If I didn't know better, I'd think I was losing my sex appeal."

The fact that she was talking to *me* about the problem meant it was already a crisis: My sophisticated, self-confident stepsister was actually developing an inferiority complex!

Palmer and I may have our differences, but down deep I really care about her.

"You must be kidding! All you have to do is look at a boy and he's your slave for life." Trying hard to keep regret out of my voice, I finished, "For example, Sam is always asking about you."

Palmer brightened. "Sam who?"

"Sam O'Leary. I got a letter from him today, and—"

"He doesn't count." She cut me off with a disgusted wave of her hand. "I hardly remember what the guy looks like."

I went dizzy with relief. Since she didn't care about Sam anymore, she couldn't possibly be hurt when I moved her out of the way to get to him!

But the expression on her face brought me down in a hurry. She was staring past me with what looked like panic in her eyes.

I swiveled my neck to determine the problem, but saw nothing out of the ordinary except a nerdy Ardie who was coming through the door of the mess hall. He waved at us, then shuffled to the other side of the room and sat down at a table.

"Do you know him?" I asked Palmer.

"He's just some senior geek who's on K.P. detail. I think his name is Holbrook Wellington." She grabbed my arm

41

and hustled me toward the front of the room with a tight, "Thanks for listening. I know you have things to do, so I won't hold you up."

"The boy situation is bound to improve soon. You're the most attractive girl in the whole camp," I assured her.

Instead of reacting to my compliment, she practically dragged me through the door. There was a strange look in her eyes when we got outside. I was so worried that I offered to skip my crafts session and help with her chores, adding, "After we finish, we'll go to the Trading Post and I'll treat you to a hot fudge sundae."

"Thanks, but chocolate gives me zits," she mumbled with a quick glance over her shoulder.

It didn't take much of my genius to see that she was trying to get rid of me. Maybe she wanted me to leave so she could cry in private, I thought, more determined than ever to cheer her up. "What you need is something to get your mind off boys. Renee and I are thinking about doing a skit for Talent Night—a takeoff on a Greek myth— and we'd love to have you in it. If you're interested, come back to the cabin after lunch and we can start writing it."

"Sounds great. You'd better hurry or you'll be late for crafts."

Since there was nothing left for me to say, I waved and started along the path. I was a third of the way to the crafts center when I remembered that I'd left my dictionary behind.

I made it back to the mess hall in thirty seconds flat, but the scene that greeted me as I entered the doorway stopped me dead in my tracks. Palmer was standing beside the tray rack flirting with Holbrook Wellington! The poor guy didn't have a chance. I could tell by the look on his face that this was the high point of his entire life.

I don't believe this, I thought. If Palmer was so insecure that she had to test her powers on that nerd, she was in much worse shape than I'd thought. Knowing she'd be mortified if she saw me watching, I backed out of the mess hall as quickly and quietly as possible, then turned to sprint across the quadrangle.

I wasn't crazy about exercise, but running would give me a chance to sort out the situation, so I decided crafts could wait. I headed for the jogging trail. During my second lap, it came to me that my stepsister wasn't the only person in trouble. What if in Palmer's current desperate condition, she decided to go after Sam again? After all, a warmed-over romance would be better than no romance at all!

Since she didn't really care about him, getting back together would be a disaster for both of them—to say nothing of me. I simply had to do something to prevent that. Turning off the track, I flopped down in the shade and began composing a letter in my head.

Dear Sam,

Your new word is the very last listing in the S section of the dictionary. It caught my eye because it has three Y's and no other vowels. It also has a secret meaning that I might share with you one of these days.

It was very sweet of you to ask about Palmer. She's having a wonderful time, and she even has a new boyfriend here at camp. His name is Holbrook something. I don't know anything about him except that he's a senior, but from his name, I would guess that he's very wealthy.

Nothing else important is going on. I'll write again soon, and next time, I'll send two *words!*

Hugs,
Georgette

TIME CAPSULE
ENTRY SIX:
BY SHANON DAVIS

———

Dear Mars,

I hate to say this, but Reid is a total creep! The way she butters Palmer up is absolutely sickening, although Palmer seems to love it. Worse than that, I've got a feeling she's interested in Rob Williams! Yesterday she and Palmer were in the back booth at the Trading Post when Rob came in. Palmer invited him to sit with them, and after they all talked for a few seconds, she got up and left Rob and Reid alone together. It may have been perfectly innocent, but it looked like a setup to me. Just in case I'm wrong, I'm not going to say anything to Lisa—yet. But I'm sure going to keep an eye on the situation.

Enough gossip—it's time for an update on Shanon Davis, the Wonder Woman of the Waves. I call myself that because every time I get in the water, I wonder if I'll get out alive! I'm making a little progress with my swimming, but I still don't trust myself anywhere near the deep end of the pool and I'm scared to death of the lake. Since Coach Barker is constantly on my case, I avoid her whenever possible. I think she probably hates me, and at the moment, I'm not too fond of her, either.

45

News bulletin! Yours truly is Camp Emerald's official roving reporter; Mr. Griffith assigned me the job of videotaping highlights of the summer session. The neatest part is that when I'm finished, he's going to make an extra copy of the tape so I can share it with you next fall!

I'd better sign off now—I have to pack my gear for tomorrow's hike. We'll be leaving at sunrise because we've got to reach the overnight campsite in the mountains before dark. I can't begin to tell you how much I wish you were here. Everyone in the cabin except me will have a partner. I won't have much time to be lonely, though. I'll be going from group to group, catching all the action with my camcorder.

Take care of your leg and give yourself a big hug for me.

Love,
Shanon

The first part of the trail up Pennacook Mountain was wide and easy, winding gently through a forest of fir, spruce, and yellow birch. The breeze smelled crisp and clean, and the ground was padded with a thick layer of pine needles. The goldenrod blooming beside the path was so gorgeous that I couldn't take the lens off of it. I moved slowly from patch to patch, filming like a maniac.

"At the rate you're going now, Shanon, you'll be out of tape by the time we reach the campsite," Mr. Griffith teased, falling in step beside me.

"I stuck in a couple of extra cassettes," I said, patting my backpack. "It's a shame that Maggie's missing all this. Isn't she feeling well?"

"She's fine, but we thought the hike might be a bit much

for little Murgatroyd or Brunhilda," he explained. "Farther along the going gets pretty rough. Perhaps I'd better take the camcorder so you won't be overloaded while you're climbing."

"That's okay. I might get some good shots on the way up."

"Don't say I didn't warn you." After a snappy salute he jogged away, calling back over his shoulder, "Go easy on the greenery and concentrate on the campers."

"Gotcha."

Not realizing that most of the group had already passed while I was busy photographing flowers, I focused the camcorder on the trail behind. Maxie and Paul, the only people in my viewfinder, were ten yards back.

The sequence I took of them would've been perfect for a perfume commercial: They were walking hand in hand, smiling at each other like there was no one else in the world.

Way to go, Max! I congratulated her silently.

Her head turned in my direction as though she'd heard me. When she spotted my camera, her face turned bright pink. "Cut that out, Shanon—I hate having my picture taken!"

"Me, too," Paul said. He jerked his hand away from Maxie's and shoved it in a pocket.

"Sorry," I mumbled, almost as flustered as they were.

"It's easy to get lost in these woods. We'd better catch up with the others," Paul said, increasing his pace to a brisk jog.

Maxie hesitated, then started after him. I gave her a thumbs-up as she trotted past me, and she sent it back with an embarrassed grin.

Shanon Davis, dedicated roving reporter, was thrilled with the video sequence; it was proof positive that Maxie and Paul had something special going. But Shanon Davis, dedicated Fox of the Third Dimension, felt guilty over invading their privacy.

After a short struggle with my conscience, I hit the rewind button and replaced Maxie and Paul with a bunch of black-eyed Susans.

I caught up with the main group just in time to catch the trail master's spiel on safety procedures.

"You'll each pair off with a hiking buddy. Secure all loose gear—you're going to need both hands free," Mr. Herzinski, Ardsley's biology instructor, barked the orders of the day. "There'll be no horsing around, no eating, no talking, no *nothing* until we get to the top. Is that clear?"

Since the man was built like Arnold Schwarzenegger, nobody was about to cross him. Grumbling under my breath, I stashed the camcorder in its leather case and slung the strap over my shoulder.

"Do you have a partner, Davis?" Coach Barker called from the edge of the crowd.

My guardian angel must have been watching out for me, because just then, Palmer hurried over to grab my arm. "You've just got to be my hiking buddy, Shanon," she pleaded, peering over her shoulder at a goony-looking Ardie who was heading in our direction. He had two knapsacks strapped on his back and was carrying a third in his hand.

Ordinarily, Palmer wouldn't have been my first pick—she would probably talk me into carrying some of her gear before it was all over. But with the swimming coach closing in on me, Palmer zoomed right to the top of the list.

I signaled Coach Barker that I already had a partner just as the goony guy shuffled up with an adoring, "Hi, Palmer. I almost lost you in the crowd."

"Holbrook-Wellington-meet-my-friend-Shanon-Davis." Palmer's introduction zipped by so fast it sounded like one long word. Before I could get in a "Hi," she rushed on, "Shanon's terribly afraid of heights, and she feels much better when I'm with her, so she begged me to be her hiking buddy."

"Okay. See you when we make camp," he said wistfully, dragging off with his load.

"Thanks for not blowing my cover, Shanon," Palmer said when he was out of earshot. "Every time I look around, Holbrook is on my heels!"

"Why don't you just tell him to get lost?"

She sighed. "I don't want to hurt the poor guy's feelings. He's got such a terrible crush on me."

The answer was a surprise. Palmer had some good qualities, but sensitivity wasn't one of them. "What happened to Reid?" I asked as the two of us got in line for the climb.

"She's with Rob—uh, Robin Whipkey." Palmer swallowed hard and a funny expression crossed her face.

I'd never heard of such a person, but I didn't really care who Reid was with as long as it wasn't me. There wasn't time for more questions anyway, because the double line of hikers started to move out.

The rocky trail narrowed and went straight up. On one side the underbrush was thick and tangled, on the other the shoulder beside the path dropped off into nothing. Well, maybe I Hollywooded that up a bit—there was a small guardrail—but it was still pretty scary. Fifteen minutes into the climb, I regretted not giving Mr. G. the camcorder. My

49

knapsack was getting heavier with every step. Palmer, who was carrying only a small tote bag and a portable radio, breezed right along.

"Where's your pack?" I puffed, wincing as my toe hit a stone.

"I'm traveling light this time."

I was tempted to ask her to carry the video camera, but I couldn't take the chance that she might drop it. We hiked until just past noon, but it seemed like the rest of my life. Just when I thought I wouldn't last another second, I heard shouts and squeals from up ahead. The front of the column had turned right and was rapidly disappearing in the space between two huge boulders. Palmer and I speeded up our pace, anxious to see what all the fuss was about.

Past the rocks, the trail became rough steps that led down into a grassy valley the size of a football stadium. Bark-covered wigwams were tucked among the trees, and directly opposite, a waterfall ran down the stone face of the mountain, ending in a sparkling pool. It was just like I always imagined the Garden of Eden would be.

When we reached the bottom of the steps, Holbrook Wellington straggled up to hand Palmer a knapsack. "I was very careful with it. I'm sure I didn't break any of your cosmetic bottles," he announced.

The scandalized look I sent her made her squirm. Dropping her gaze to the toes of her shoes, she mumbled, "Thanks a lot for volunteering to carry my stuff, Holbrook."

"I was glad to do it," he assured her. "Wanna go with me to look at the waterfall?"

"I've got to rest for a while, but I'll catch up with you later this afternoon," she promised.

I waited until he'd left before I exploded. "How could you take advantage of him like that? It was terrible for you to make him haul your junk up that steep trail!"

"If he doesn't mind, why should you?" she said airily.

"Because—" I never finished because Maxie came over to us with our sleeping assignments. "Georgette and Renee are in wigwam one with three other girls, and we Foxes plus Reid are bunking together in number four," she announced. "Let's go drop our stuff and change into bathing suits. Last one in the swimming hole is a dirty sweat sock!"

I felt a familiar churning in my stomach, but I pasted on a sickly grin and followed her and Palmer to our wigwam. Amy and Reid were already settled in.

The inside of the bark hut wasn't fancy, but there was enough space for the five of us to move around without stepping on each other. The place was lit by a battery-operated lantern, and a bunch of bedrolls were stacked in the back.

"Surely they don't expect me to sleep in this hole," Palmer said.

"You can always take your sleeping bag outside. I'm sure the bears wouldn't mind having you for a roommate," Amy teased.

Palmer shut up and started digging through her knapsack.

"Aren't you going to change, Shanon?" Maxie piped up.

"With all the extra videocassettes, I didn't have enough room to pack a swim suit," I lied.

"I brought along a spare you can borrow," Palmer said, tossing me a French-cut backless number.

"Uh—thanks, but I don't think it's my color," I said

51

quickly. Then before anyone could argue I snatched up the camcorder and ran out the door of the hut.

This is ridiculous, I told myself. *You, Shanon Davis, are turning into a complete chicken! You can't let your fear of the water take over your whole life.* I decided then and there that I was going to learn to swim if it killed me. But not today. And maybe not tomorrow, either.

There was no way to escape from my phobia. Everyone at the campsite was aimed straight for the swimming hole, so that's where I had to go to take my pictures. They all seemed to be having major fun—splashing, laughing, dunking each other. The more I filmed the scene the more depressed I got. I'd be having a good time, too, if I weren't such a baby!

Taking a wide detour around the spot where Coach Barker was giving a class to some of the younger girls, I headed for the other side of the pool. Amy, Nikos, and Mr. Griffith had just gotten out of the water and were soaking up the rays of the late-afternoon sun.

"Say cheese," I commanded. panning the camera across the trio.

"You're doing great work, Shanon," said Mr. Griffith. "It takes a lot of discipline to stick to a job while everyone else is having fun." He stood up and stretched. "Speaking of which, I'm going in for one last dip before dinner."

He entered the water with an effortless jackknife dive, not surfacing until he was ten yards away from the shore.

Sighing with envy, I sat down next to Amy.

"We're talking about the exercises we'll have to do during the survival weekend," she told me.

"They're pretty standard—a race over an obstacle

course, endurance tests—easy stuff like that," Nikos explained.

"Easy for you, maybe," I said.

Amy's eyes danced with excitement. "At the end, we get to spend an entire day in a cavern."

"I don't think it's such a hot idea," Nikos objected.

That was my opinion, too, but I kept it to myself. It could have been a trick of the fading light, but it seemed to me that his face went a shade pale.

"Why?" Amy asked, frowning.

John Adams walked up to put in his grumpy two cents worth. "Because the girls can't pull it off. I'll bet you you'll all freak out the minute you see a bat."

Amy gave him a disgusted look. "Girls are just as brave as boys," she said coldly.

"John's only kidding," Nikos interrupted, reaching over to tickle her nose with a strand of her wet hair. "You're so cute when you go into your women's lib mode."

"If you had one ounce of sensitivity, you wouldn't say a macho, chauvinist thing like that." Amy pushed his hand away and rose to her feet. Dismissing the guys with an annoyed grunt, she turned and dove into the water.

Nikos hesitated a few seconds before he jumped in behind her. He caught up easily, and though I couldn't hear what they were saying, I guessed that he was trying to apologize. She dunked him, he returned the favor, then they both came up laughing again.

John's face was fixed in a scowl as he watched the scene. *Jealousy makes people weird*, I thought as he stalked away without a glance in my direction. Before John and Amy broke up, he'd been such a nice guy.

By now the sun was setting, and hungry campers began

53

to home in on the huge fire Mr. Herzinski had built in the center of the valley. It's amazing how good food is when it's cooked over an open fire. My first hot dog slipped off the stick and fell into the ashes, but when I rescued it, it still tasted better than anything I'd ever eaten. After two more, plus potato chips and a cold soda, I was so stuffed I could barely move.

But duty and my camcorder called. Everywhere I focused there were terrific shots: Mr. G. with a smear of mustard on his chin, Amy feeding Nikos a roasted marshmallow, Reid Olivier snuggling up to Rob Williams, Georgette and—

Reid Olivier snuggling up to Rob Williams???

I panned the camera back so quickly I nearly got a crook in my neck. Sure enough, the two of them were sitting so close that a sheet of paper wouldn't have fit between them! I went from hot to cold and back again, so mad that steam was practically coming out of my ears. Having Reid for a roommate was bad enough, but I sure wasn't going to let her get away with snatching Lisa's boyfriend.

Since I couldn't very well order her to stay away from Rob, I decided to approach the problem from the other side. Walking over to where they were sitting, I trained my lens on Rob's face. "Hold that pose." Working to keep my tone light, I stuck in a casual, "Have you heard from Lisa lately?"

"Not since last week." He blushed and ducked his head.

"I write her almost every day. I wish she could have come to camp with us," I pressed on.

"We all miss Lisa. She's so sweet and funny and considerate," Reid cooed, quickly shifting the subject to: "Could you go get me another cola, Robbie? All that climbing and swimming has made me so thirsty."

He scrambled up like he had springs in his feet. After he was gone, Reid rose to face me, her eyes narrow and snake-mean. "If you're trying to guilt Rob out, it won't work," she warned. "He doesn't care about Lisa."

"That's not true," I protested. "They've been pen pals for ages, and they write each other all the time."

"Yeah, and she's always complaining about the stupid fights her parents have. Rob's going to dump her because he's totally sick of reading all those whiny letters."

Shock made me suck in a sharp breath. "I don't believe that!"

"It doesn't matter what you believe, Miss Goody-Goody Chicken. He's with me now, and there's nothing you can do about it."

I hated Reid Olivier. Worse than that, I hated myself for not having the guts to punch her lights out. Helpless with anger, I spun on my heel and stalked away.

TIME CAPSULE
ENTRY SEVEN:
BY MAXIE SCHLOSS

Dear Maxie,
   What has a bad case of insomnia, wears gold false teeth, and uses a noose for a necktie? If you want to know the answer to the riddle, meet me down by the boathouse after life-saving class.

Love,
Paul

The class of expert swimmers was waiting for Coach Barker to start the advanced session. Paul was horsing around with a bunch of guys, and I sat glued to a spot on the other side of the pool, unable to work up enough nerve to go over and ask him about the note I'd found tucked in the side pocket of my tote bag. Except for the magic minute Shanon caught with her camcorder, Paul and I hadn't been very close during the overnight hike. There were always a lot of people around, and as I mentioned before, we didn't do well together when we were in crowds. But that was okay, because when we were holding hands on the trail up the mountain, the look in his eyes told me how he felt about me.

I was puzzling over the meaning of the mysterious riddle when a blast from Coach Barker's whistle jerked me to attention.

"We're now going to practice the cross-chest rescue carry. Our make-believe victim for today is"—she paused to run down the list on her clipboard, then announced—"Maxie Schloss."

I groaned at the bad news; pretending to be drowning was everyone's least favorite thing to do. Since I was stuck with the job, though, I was determined to be a world-class victim. For the next forty minutes, I splashed around the center of the pool giving my would-be rescuers a hard time. If the situation had been for real, I would have been a goner—none of the swimmers could even get near me.

By the time Paul's turn came around, I was a little winded, but I couldn't afford to let up; the other kids would have thought I was trying to make him look good. He reached my side in four powerful strokes and, neatly ducking my pinwheeling arms, tried to slip his hand across my chest.

Flipping over on my stomach, I threw my arms around his shoulders and dragged him under the surface of the water.

The move must have caught him by surprise; he struggled against me, hands flapping, legs thrashing. Then without any warning he went limp and still.

What was wrong with him?

His body drifted downward. I grabbed for his arm, but it slipped out of my grasp. Before I knew what was happening, he was lying spread-eagled on the bottom of the pool.

At first I wasn't too worried—Paul was really good at holding his breath underwater. But when a gush of bubbles came from his mouth, I panicked. Maybe he was having some kind of attack!

Fighting off the fear that was exploding inside my head, I bounced up for a huge gulp of air, then went down after him. When I touched his shoulder, he rolled away from me, his eyes tightly closed. I reached for him again and it seemed like forever until I got a grip on his hair. Kicking desperately against the weight of the water, I somehow managed to haul him up, praying hard with every stroke. If Paul drowned because of my fooling around, I wouldn't want to live, either. Finally we reached the surface. I treaded water frantically while I supported his head.

"Please don't be dead, Paul," I gasped.

His eyes popped open and he grinned. "Gotcha!"

The burst of applause from the sides of the pool told me the whole thing had been an act.

"You jerk!" I spluttered, laughing.

Before I knew what was happening, he had yanked me into the cross-chest carry position and was sidestroking into shallow water.

"Both of you deserve high marks for that performance," Coach Barker told us as Paul dragged me up on the deck. Turning to the rest of the class, she continued, "The next exercise is a demonstration of mouth-to-mouth resuscitation. Do I have any volunteers?"

"Let Maxie and Paul do it," someone at the back of the crowd yelled out.

"Yeah—they've probably been practicing the technique already," another swimmer said, hooting with laughter. "I'll bet they've got it down pat!"

The rest of the class greeted that statement with whistles, hoots, and loud oooooo's. Paul backed away from me immediately, his face a bright crimson.

Of course, he wasn't the only one dying of embarrassment. Luckily, the alarm on Coach Barker's watch buzzed, ending the session. "We'll put off the demonstration until tomorrow," she said briskly.

Paul didn't look at me, but he mumbled, "See you at the boathouse in ten minutes, Maxie."

By the time I'd dashed through the locker-room shower and slipped into my clothes, my nerves had pulled themselves back together—sort of. My heart was thumping hard, though, as I trotted down the path to the landing.

When I arrived at the dock, Paul was stowing canvas bags in a small canoe.

Avoiding his gaze, I mumbled, "What's all that stuff?"

"Mostly food. After we get to the other side of the lake, there's still a pretty fair walk ahead. We'll probably get hungry along the way."

A picnic in the woods with Paul was too radical to be believed! Throttling my excitement down to a low roar, I glanced around the deserted pier. "Shouldn't we ask someone before we go out?"

"Mr. Herzinski said it'd be okay since we're both advanced swimmers. I told him we'd stick to the shallows and get back by dinnertime."

Paul steadied the boat and as I climbed into the bow, I reached for one of the paddles.

"I know the way, and it'll be easier if I do the paddling on the way over," he objected.

I shrugged and settled in the seat so I'd be facing him. "Where are we going?"

He flashed a mysterious smile. "To the Twilight Zone."

"Aren't you going to give me the answer to the riddle?"

"Not until we get there," he said, pushing off from the shore.

Paul usually meant exactly what he said, so there was no point in pressing the subject. Neither one of us said anything for a while. There was only the sound of the canoe moving through the water.

When we reached the halfway point around the shoreline, Paul stopped paddling and asked, "Were you serious when you told Shanon you hated having your picture taken?"

"Not really—she just caught me by surprise," I answered, turning pink.

"Would you mind if I took a couple of shots of you now? You look terrific with the wind blowing your hair around."

With a lead-in like that, how could I refuse?

Paul secured his paddle, took a Nikon from his knapsack, and began adjusting the settings on the camera.

"You must be seriously into photography," I said, staring into the high-tech lens. "That's an awesome camera."

"My parents have a photo-journalist friend who works for *Life* magazine. He gave it to me when I was a kid," Paul explained. "He also helped me to set up a darkroom at home so I can do my own developing."

I was definitely impressed. "I guess since your dad's the

CEO of an automobile company, you must get to meet a lot of important people." I couldn't believe I'd said that. It popped out of my mouth before I could stop it. "Sorry," I said, "that was a dumb thing for me to say—particularly since I know how much I hate it when people talk about my father being a television comedian. It gets kind of weird growing up with famous parents, doesn't it?"

"You've got that right. A lot of times I wish my dad were someone ordinary—like a truck driver or a mailman," Paul agreed, clicking away. "Other kids are always asking me how it feels to have my pick of the cars in our factory."

That one hadn't occurred to me, and I couldn't hold back the question, "Which model do you have?"

"A foot-mobile until I turn eighteen and save up enough money to buy my own car. And even then, I won't get any kind of discount—dad says I'll appreciate things more if I have to work for them." He put his camera away and started paddling again. "Actually," he said, "I have to admit that my parents act pretty normal most of the time. We always go on family vacations together, and when I'm home from school, I hang out in mom's studio. Once in a while, she even uses some of my work in the children's books she illustrates."

"That's neat." I trailed my fingers along in the water, enjoying the closeness between us. This was the most Paul had ever told me about himself. "Are you going to be an artist when you grow up?"

He shook his head. "A doctor, probably, or at least some kind of scientist."

"Me, too," I said, nearly exploding with happiness. It was incredible how much we had in common. I was in the midst of a fantasy about setting up a practice with him when the hull of the canoe thudded against the shore.

"This is it," Paul told me, leaving the boat to secure the bow line on a post that was sticking out from the ground.

I stepped out onto the rocky stretch of beach and shivered. I couldn't explain it, but an uneasy feeling was sneaking up on me. Somehow the air seemed heavier on this side of the lake, so still that all I could hear was the ripple of waves washing over the sand. And it seemed a lot gloomier, too—maybe because a tall, thick stand of trees was blocking out most of the afternoon sun.

Paul handed me one knapsack, then slung the other over his shoulder, moving off into the woods without a word. It was hard going for a while; brambly bushes crowded the faint path we were following, and the ground sloped upward at a steep angle.

After fifteen minutes of steady climbing, Paul slowed his pace. "Are we there?" I asked, puffing a little.

"Yep." He pushed his way through a patch of sumac, holding aside the branches so I could get through.

We came out into a large, uneven clearing that was circled by pine trees. Opposite us, a two-story stone house stood in the middle of an overgrown lawn. The front door hung crazily from one hinge and the two paneless windows on the second floor stared down at us like the empty eyes of a skull.

A shiver of dread raced up my spine. "You weren't kidding when you said we were on our way to the Twilight Zone! What is this place?"

"Mr. Griffith mentioned it the other night when some of the guys were telling ghost stories," Paul said, grinning smugly.

"Ghost stories?"

"There's a spooky legend about this place. It's probably not true, but it's fun. I'll fill you in while we're eating," he promised, leading the way to a weed-free spot under an oak tree.

While we sat sharing cranberry juice from Paul's Thermos and the seemingly endless supply of peanut butter and jelly sandwiches he'd packed, he began the story. "Right before the Revolutionary War, the place belonged to Thaddeus Blackthorn, the richest and greediest man in New Hampshire. He had so much money that—"

"—he had his dentist make him a set of gold false teeth," I guessed, remembering Paul's note.

"Right. He was also a double agent who was paid by the British to help them set a trap for a band of Minutemen operating in the next village. But his daughter, Charity, had a thing for one of the Patriots, and when she slipped out to warn her boyfriend, one of the Redcoat guards shot her. Pops was so broken up that he hanged himself—that's the noose necktie part of the riddle." Paul demolished half his sandwich in two bites, then finished, "Now for the insomnia: The scoop is that old Thad still walks around the house moaning and groaning every time there's a full moon."

"Lovely," I said.

He slipped an arm around my shoulders. "You don't believe in ghosts, do you?"

"Course not." I gulped, peering warily at the building as I added, "But as future scientists, we have to keep an open mind about these things."

"Definitely," he agreed. "We have to keep an open mind about a lot of things."

Before I could figure out what all that meant, he took my face between his hands and guided my lips to meet his.

We hadn't kissed in a while, and—I know this sounds dumb—at first I just worried about technique. I wasn't sure whether or not to hold my breath. And I didn't quite know what to do with my arms, so I sort of clamped them around Paul's neck. But I passed the awkward stage real quick—his mouth was so warm and sweet I stopped thinking about everything else. One of the things I'd read about kissing was definitely true: The clock *did* go into slow motion. As I snuggled against him, every second seemed to lengthen into an hour. The spicy shampoo smell of his hair made me light-headed, and when his fingers started to trace a path down the side of my cheek . . .

I pulled away from him, my pulse beating like a berserk tom-tom. "We'd better head back now. It must be getting close to dinnertime," I stammered, avoiding his eyes.

"I guess so." His voice had gone way down to husky and it was as shaky as mine. "Want to explore the haunted house before we go?"

I glanced toward the stone building, and the spooky feeling I'd had when we first reached the shore came back full force. "Not while I'm still alive!" I said, scrambling up.

"At least let me take a picture of you standing in front of it," Paul said.

My "Okay" was very reluctant. I edged over to a spot that was ten yards from the front porch, peering back over my shoulder as I turned to face the camera. I wasn't too crazy abut having my back to the place.

"Relax—old Thaddeus only comes out at night," Paul teased. After the first shot, he pulled a collapsible tripod from his knapsack and arranged it with the camera on top.

"What are you doing now?" I asked, fidgeting.

"Setting the self-timing cycle. I want to get a picture of us together." When he had finished fiddling with the lens, he dashed across the clearing. Just before the shutter clicked, he slipped his arm around my waist and pulled me close to him.

Even when the photograph had been taken, we didn't move.

Paul brushed his lips across my forehead, whispering, "Maxie, I—"

The rest of the sentence was interrupted by a series of "whuffs" that stretched out into a weird groan. "Paul," I said, "that sound . . . it's coming from the house!"

Paul's face turned a sickly white. Then he grabbed my hand and we raced across the clearing, catching the tripod and camera on the fly. Forget the knapsacks—we didn't stop running until we reached the shore of Emerald Lake!

By the time we'd launched the canoe, though, our nerves had begun to settle down. "That was probably the sound of the wind whistling through the chimney," I said with a tight giggle.

"Probably."

This time we both paddled, moving the boat along with swift, smooth strokes.

"We really should have gone in to see where that noise was coming from," Paul said after a while.

"You're right. If we're going to be scientists, we have to be objective—even when things get scary," I agreed.

"Maybe next week we should check it out again."

Crazy as it was, I liked the idea of going back to the haunted house with Paul. It was something that seemed to

65

belong just to the two of us. As I turned to glance back at the brooding forest, pure happiness flooded my chest. Haunted or not, I thought Thaddeus Blackthorn's house the most wonderful place in the whole state of New Hampshire.

TIME CAPSULE
ENTRY EIGHT:
BY AMY HO

Love is major trouble and romance is just a myth.
I'm fed up to my teeth with boys, especially Nikos Smith!
He's a fourteen-karat oinker, a muscle-headed goon.
The next time he comes near me, I'll send him to the moon.
CHORUS: *Sisters of the world unite—*
               Let's do away with guys!
               They're loud-mouthed,
                   bragging, macho geeks
               Who all belong in sties!

    The afternoon I wrote that song was the absolute pits—capitalized, underlined, and with three exclamation points at the end. It was also the beginning of a war that nearly blew Camp Emerald apart.

    The worst part was that the day started out to be a real winner. When the Avengers came out of the dugout, the temperature was in the low seventies, the wind was calm, and the stands were jammed: absolutely perfect conditions for the first game of the softball tournament. I was about to jog out to the pitcher's mound when Nikos pulled me aside.

"Is the arm okay? How are you feeling? Have you got all the signals straight?" His questions tumbled over each other.

"Fine—great—yes," I answered, grinning at him as I added, "You can relax. This game is already in the win column."

I wasn't just boasting. My prediction came from a deep-down, sure-as-sunrise feeling that we couldn't lose. I had dreamed about the game all night, and just before I woke up, the final score had flashed into my mind: The Avengers would trash the Ninja Turtles two to zero.

"I'm not expecting miracles." Nikos looked really worried as he pleaded, "Just give it your best shot."

"I always do," I told him.

He seemed not to have heard me. "It's not going to be an easy win. Sherman's out with a virus, so I've got to start Renee Quick," he announced glumly. "Her fielding is lousy and she can't bat worth a dime."

"She's got a lot of heart, though," I said. "Come on, Nikos—lighten up, will you? We're supposed to be having fun!"

Nikos frowned. "Easy for you to say. If Phyllis McGill's team beats the Avengers, the guys will never let me live it down."

Something about the statement hit me wrong, but before I could figure out what, the senior Ardie who was acting as the director of the tournament yelled, "Play ball!"

"I'm really nervous," Renee confided as we trotted out on the field. "If I mess up, Nikos is going to blow a gasket."

"You'll do fine, but just for insurance, you can borrow my good luck piece." Without breaking my stride, I un-

68

fastened the gold barrette I was wearing and handed it to her, explaining, "My uncle gave it to me, and it always works. The design in the center is a Chinese character that means victory."

"Thanks, but won't you need it?"

"Not today," I answered confidently.

Before the Ninja Turtles knew what was happening, the first inning was history. I'd retired all three of their batters with sizzling strikes.

"Way to go," Nikos said as I trotted in from the mound. Before I could react to his congratulations, he turned to one of the guys with the order, "Peter, get in there and pinch hit for Barbara."

Taking our third base-person out at that particular moment didn't make much sense to me—Barbara was a fairly good player. But I figured Nikos must have some strategy in mind, so I didn't question him. In fact, I was too pumped up to think of anything except pitching. Though I hadn't even reached top form yet, my reflexes were razor-sharp and the muscles in my body were working in absolute harmony—Amy Ho was a lean, mean pitching machine!

My batting was another matter, though; I struck out every time I came up to the plate. The rest of the Avengers were also in a slump, and the score stayed knotted at zero-zero.

After I'd struck out six more Turtles, Nikos wrapped me in a bear hug. "You're absolutely fantastic!"

For a moment I thought I'd died and gone to heaven—he was actually proud of me! Although I was kind of embarrassed because practically the whole camp was watching, being in his arms was the most wonderful feeling I'd ever had.

I blushed as I pulled away. "I guess I'm doing okay."

"You're working on a no-hitter, babe. This one will go down in Camp Emerald's record book!" he said, giving me a smile that sent shivers up my back.

I'd been too busy pitching to give it much thought. "I wish you hadn't said that," I gulped.

Nikos didn't answer. Swiveling away from me, he told Rob to go in for Jennifer.

As the game headed into the next inning, I noticed the rising chant, "Amy—Amy—Amy!" and when I turned to scan the crowd, my cabin mates jumped up to start a wave that rippled through the packed bleachers. My knees were rubbery when I walked out to the mound—which was peculiar, because my nerves were as tight as the strings on my guitar.

I had trouble with the next two batters—it took six pitches each before I finally struck them out. And then John Adams stalked up to the plate, the expression on his face grim. When my first pitch whistled too close to his kneecap, he jumped back angrily.

"Watch it! Are you trying to bean me on purpose?" he growled.

"Sorry," I apologized, shaken by the nasty tone of his question. I gritted my teeth and went into my windup. The second the softball left my hand, I knew I had blown the throw.

John's bat connected with a loud crack and the ball sailed up into the glare of the sun. A moan came from the stands.

"I'll get it," Renee yelled from the outfield.

Considering her past performance, there was no chance that she would catch that pop fly. The scene shifted into slow motion as she backpedaled, launched herself into the air, and stretched out her arm. By some miracle, the ball dropped neatly into the center of her glove. The crowd went wild, and so did I—Renee Quick had saved my no-hitter!

My excitement lasted all of two minutes. When Renee and I got back to the bench, Nikos was setting the batting lineup for the sixth inning. "George can substitute for Renee and I'll go in for Amy," he told Rob briskly.

My mouth dropped open in disbelief as I finally picked up the pattern. One by one, Nikos had eliminated the girls on the team from the roster: During the last inning, the Avengers would field a nearly all-male team! "If you pinch-hit for me, I can't go back in the game," I protested. "It isn't fair to take me out when I'm working on a no-hitter!"

"Sorry about that, but you've lost your concentration," Nikos said stubbornly.

"But we don't have another good pitcher," I reminded him.

"I can handle it."

The hidden meaning behind what he was saying began to sink in. "Are you telling me that even though your elbow is hurt, you still think you can pitch better than me?"

He touched my shoulder, his eyes apologetic. "I have to do this for the good of the team, but I want you to know you've done an excellent job. For a girl, you've got one of the best pitching arms I've ever seen."

I jerked away from his hand, so mad I was seeing double. "If I were a guy, you'd let me finish the game."

The guilty flush on his face told me I was dead on target.

"If you were a guy, you'd be able to handle the pressure better," Nikos said stiffly.

There was one more thing I needed to know. "Why have you been substituting guys for all the girls on the team?"

"Bottom line, we need runs, and you girls can't get them for us," he admitted.

"Bottom line, you're an insensitive macho clod!" I snapped. "We haven't gotten any hits yet, but neither have you guys."

By now, some of the Ninja Turtles were drifting over to see what was holding up the game. Maxie, Paul Grant, Palmer, and Shanon had left the stands and were hurrying in my direction.

"Chill out, Amy. We can talk about this later," Nikos warned, his face darkening.

"We'll talk about it right now!" Nearly ready to explode, I moved closer to him. "On my worst days, I'm twice the softball player you'll ever be, Nikos Smith."

"Get real, *Ms.* Ho—everyone knows that girls aren't as good at sports as boys," John Adams piped up.

"You keep out of this," I hissed.

"Don't let them get to you, Amy. Nikos and John are definitely a minority—most guys don't think that way," Maxie spoke up. She glanced at Paul as though she were waiting for him to back her, but he didn't say a word.

Rob cleared his throat hesitantly. "I'm not putting you down, Amy, but it's a physical fact that girls aren't as strong or as fast as guys."

That piece of drivel brought murmurs of agreement from every male in the crowd. It also drew boos from all the girls.

"Or as much nerve," John added. "I bet every single one

of you chickens out during the survival weekend. I can just see you fainting dead away when you walk into that cave."

Nikos stiffened, then cut off the discussion with a flick of his hand. "Let's just get back to the game," he said shortly.

"As far as I'm concerned, this game is history," I told him. "I'm not going to play with people who don't have sense enough to appreciate my talent."

Renee stepped up beside me "That goes for me, too."

"And us," Jennifer and Barbara joined in.

"Since you no longer have enough players to field a team, Nikos, the Avengers will have to forfeit the game," Phyllis McGill crowed from the sidelines.

The word "forfeit" wasn't even in Nikos's vocabulary. His face darkened with anger. "This is all your fault, Amy, and it just proves the point that girls are a bunch of quitters. Whenever things don't go your way, you start whining."

"Oh, yeah? Well, since you're into proving points, check this one out," I stormed, raking him with a scathing glance. "I'm challenging you to a softball game—girls against boys. We'll show you who's the weaker sex!"

"You're on." His eyes narrowed to mere slits. "We'll wipe up the field with you."

His scorn cut right through me, but I'd have died before I let him know it. "I'd expect that from a Neanderthal loser who roots for the Chicago Cubs. And I—"

KABOOOOOOOMMMM! An earsplitting blast of thunder cut off the rest of the insult I was about to hurl at him. We'd all been so involved in the argument that we hadn't noticed a fast-moving storm tracking in from the west. The sun was gone in two minutes flat, streaks of lightning tore the clouds, and quarter-sized splashes of water hit the ground. Most campers split the scene immediately, but Nikos and I just stood glaring at each other.

The rain was cooling my temper and I was beginning to regret a few of the things I'd said to him. I had gone a bit overboard with the name-calling. I guess he was having second thoughts about the situation, too, because for a split second, he looked as though he were about to apologize.

Then his dark eyes grew hard. "I thought we had something good going, Amy. But you embarrassed me in front of all my friends—I'll never forgive you for that." Jaw clenched tight, he spun on his heel and stalked off.

As I slogged away from the softball field, I was so numb I didn't even feel the wind and water lashing against me. The storm kept my mind off my misery, so I just kept walking. Twenty minutes later I was totally soaked, but it didn't matter. At least I had a legitimate excuse for my wet face—no one could tell that I'd been crying.

I might have lost the guy I was nuts about, but the other Foxes hadn't deserted me. When I dragged myself through the door of the cabin, they crowded around me sympathetically. Dry clothes and good friends did wonders for my morale. And with dinnertime fast approaching, I was beginning to feel like my normal self again.

"Before I'm through with Nikos Smith, he'll wish he'd never seen a softball," I vowed. "We're going to wipe up the diamond with those geeks."

My cabin mates were silent.

"What's wrong?" I asked. "You do think we can win, don't you?"

Maxie shrugged. "Not really, but we can give it a shot."

"We're in," Georgette and Renee said in unison.

"Might as well," Palmer agreed.

Shanon sighed. "I'd probably be more of a handicap than a help—you know how bad I am at sports."

"We'll all coach you," I promised, turning to glance across the room. "How about you, Reid?"

She looked up from the magazine she was reading. "I hurt my wrist playing tennis a couple of months ago. Count me out."

That suited me just fine—I'd only asked her to be polite.

"Now that that's all settled, let's go to dinner. I'm starving," Palmer complained.

The storm had fizzled out as we headed across the quadrangle to the mess hall. I lagged behind the others; Nikos and his cabin mates were assigned to a table directly behind ours. The prospect of seeing him had killed my appetite.

The first shock of the evening was that while we were going through the serving line, all the girls in the room gave me a standing ovation. The second was a banner tacked to the wall. Printed on it in bold letters was **"Women—The Weaker Sex!!"**

"I'll bet anything Nikos made that," I muttered, setting my tray on our table with a thump that rattled the dishes. I glared in his direction, but he was busy talking to John.

"He's just trying to get your goat. Ignore it," Maxie said.

I tried to follow her advice, but while I picked over my spaghetti and meatballs, I was doing a slow burn. I could almost feel Nikos's cold stare boring into the spot between my shoulder blades.

The sensation was more than I could take. I was twisting

in my seat to look at him when a garlic roll zinged past. It missed me by inches, landing in Palmer's lap.

"Of all the nerve!" she exclaimed. Scooping up the piece of bread, she turned to hurl it back at the boys' table.

"Food fight—food fight," a voice across the room yelled.

In nothing flat, the air in the mess hall was filled with flying bits of dinner. When a slice of tomato from someone's salad splattered against my face, the frustration and anger that had been building all day suddenly came to a boil. Before I could stop myself, I snatched up my plate, marched back to Nikos's table, and dumped the entire serving of spaghetti over his head. The mess hall exploded with hoots of laughter.

Not bothering to wipe off the tomato sauce that was dripping down his cheeks, Nikos asked in a deadly calm voice, "Why did you do that?"

"You wanted a war, you got one!" Before he could launch a counterstrike, I whirled and ran from the mess hall.

If I live to be a hundred, I'll never forget the expression on his face, a combination of shock, humiliation, and, above all, hurt. For a second I was tempted to go back and apologize, but I knew in my heart it was useless. Nothing I could possibly say would heal the split between us.

TIME CAPSULE
ENTRY NINE:
BY SHANON DAVIS

Dear Mars,

News flash from the battle zone: *In the wake of the spaghetti incident, the war between the sexes is heating up. Amy Ho, leader of the Foxy Feminist Forces, issued a recent statement that accuses the enemy of short-sheeting the beds in Cabin F. General Nikos Smith, commander in chief of the Ardsley Oinkers, denies responsibility for the covert attack, and blames the F.F.F. for the mysterious noises that are keeping his army awake all night. There seems to be no possibility of a truce, and it is feared that both sides will suffer heavy casualties. An unnamed source (whose initials are K.M.) indicates that the camp administration is currently considering radical measures to bring about a cease-fire.*

Being a war correspondent is a lot more exciting than working as a plain old camp reporter, but I have to admit, I'll be glad when this hassle blows over. Amy believes we're fighting for the pride and dignity of women, and she says if we win the game, we could become a symbol of hope for girls all over the country. Personally,

I think she's overreacting, but it would hurt her feelings if I said so.

She made us promise to ignore the Ardies until this thing is settled once and for all. Maxie is very unhappy about it, and I can't really blame her. She and Paul were getting along really well before the whole mess started. So far, they haven't broken the no-speaking rule, but I'm not sure how much longer they can hold out. Lucky for me you're not here—I positively couldn't stand not being able to talk to you!

This may sound incredible, but Palmer's all for the "Ban the Boys" policy. She keeps insisting that she's not into guys anymore—can you believe that? She spends most of her time with Reid, Georgette, and Renee because they're trying to work out an act for Talent Night. Palmer and Georgette are actually getting along these days, but the rest of us don't think the change is permanent. I'll let you know when, where, and how the battling Durands "resume hostilities," as we say in the news business!

The girls' team is practicing at least three hours a day to get in shape for the challenge, and between practices, we eat, sleep, and breathe strategy. I'm really beginning to hate softball—not as much as I do swimming, though. As I mentioned before, I've been going out of my way to duck Coach Barker. Well, yesterday my luck ran out. She cornered me at lunch, and I couldn't get away until I'd promised to meet her at the lakefront this afternoon for a private lesson. Isn't that grim? It'll be after the regular class is over, so at least none of the other kids will see me make a fool of myself.

Just in case I drown, I want you to remember that I think you're the sweetest, neatest, sunniest, funniest guy in

*the whole wide world! (I would have stuck in cutest, but I
couldn't think of another adjective that rhymed with it.)*

> *Double hugs and triple love,
> Shanon*

I was standing at the Trading Post cash register, waiting
to buy a stamp for my letter to Mars, when the other Foxes
rushed in and jerked me out of line.

"You won't believe what those goons have done!" Amy
rasped.

Palmer's face was pale with rage. "I've never been so
humiliated in my entire life!"

"What's happened now?" I sighed, steeling myself for
the latest. "They didn't put a skunk in our cabin, did
they?"

"No, but now that you mention it, there must be hun-
dreds of those furry little stink bombs running around
in the woods. If we could think of some way to catch
one . . ." Amy trailed off, a calculating gleam in her eyes.

"If you're thinking what I think you're thinking, forget
it!" Maxie squawked. "I'm not about to go skunk hunting
just so you can get even with Nikos."

"After this last attack, that terrorist deserves anything
we can dream up," Palmer sided with Amy. "I know someone who might be willing to trap a skunk and sneak it
through the guys' window for us. All I have to do is—"

"We're not going to use an innocent animal—period,
exclamation point, end of discussion," I cut her off. "Now,
will somebody tell me what happened?"

"You've got to see it for yourself," Maxie said, taking
my arm to hustle me from the Trading Post.

A crowd of hooting, cackling Ardies had collected outside in the quadrangle, and as we tried to push our way through, someone yelled out, "Yo, Amy—camouflage is really kinky! Do you do your shopping at an army surplus store?"

Before I could ask what the guy meant, Amy went off. She might have done some serious damage if Maxie and Palmer hadn't grabbed her before she could get to him.

"Break it up," Mr. Griffith commanded, striding into the middle of the gathering. "You guys get on about your business and leave the girls alone."

As the boys shuffled off, laughing and mumbling to each other, Amy turned on Mr. G. with fire in her eyes. "We're perfectly able to take care of ourselves."

I expected him to level her for talking to him like that, but he only smiled. "I know. I was trying to protect the Ardies," he teased. The humor on his face faded as he said, "You can take down your—er—belongings, now. And don't even think of going for revenge. Your little war is getting out of hand, and it's got to stop right here. Do I make myself clear?"

Amy nodded obediently, and apparently satisfied that the matter was settled, Mr. G. walked away.

"Will somebody please tell me what's going on?" I begged.

Maxie turned to point silently at the bulletin board in the middle of the lawn.

Four sets of underwear—tops and bottoms—were tacked up for all the world to see. Over each one was a label identifying its owner: of the seven people in our cabin, only Georgette, Renee, and Reid had been spared the embarrassment.

If I could've found a hole to crawl into, I would've gone below forever. As it was, I reached the bulletin board in two seconds flat, shaking with anger as I retrieved my underwear. After the short-sheeting incident, we'd decided to take turns watching the cabin so the guys couldn't sneak in, but our sentry system obviously wasn't working. "Reid was supposed to be on guard duty this afternoon. Where is she?" I growled.

"She's with—uh—she had to help Mrs. Butter in the camp kitchen," Palmer explained, a peculiar expression crossing her face.

"It seems very strange that none of her undies were stolen," I said suspiciously.

"I'll get even with Nikos Smith if it's the last thing I do," Amy muttered as she removed the thumbtacks that were holding her camouflage-patterned panties to the cork.

"Mr. Griffith said we had to drop it," I reminded her.

She scowled at me. "We can't trust him anymore—he's one of *them*!" With that, she linked arms with Palmer and marched back toward our cabin.

"If this doesn't stop soon, someone could really get hurt," I said to Maxie. "While I'm taking my swimming lesson, please don't let Amy and Palmer do anything stupid."

"I've got it covered. You just concentrate on staying afloat." She punched my shoulder lightly, smiling encouragement. "If you just relax, you'll have a lot of fun in the water."

"Right." As I dragged myself down to the cabana and changed into my bathing suit, I forgot all about the silly underwear episode. Compared to the prospect of a watery death, having my personal things displayed in public was no big deal.

Coach Barker was waiting for me at the lakefront, her usually businesslike face softened by a smile. "Before we begin, let's talk for a minute," she said, patting a space beside her on the sand. When I was settled, she asked, "When's the first time you can remember being afraid of the water?"

I thought for a moment. "When I was five. I was at the beach with my parents and I got stung by a jellyfish," I answered, shuddering as the experience grew more vivid in my head.

"That must have been terrible for you," she sympathized. "And ever since, you've been afraid to learn to swim?"

"I already know how—at least, I did once. My father taught me when I was just a baby, and he tells me that I used to love it." I let out a deep sigh. "Now every time I get into anything deeper than a bathtub, I start thinking about what might be lurking on the bottom."

"Would you rather take this lesson in the pool?"

"That wouldn't help. I know it's dumb, but I always imagine that squiggly things are hiding in the drain pipes."

"It's not dumb to be afraid, but the fear doesn't have to control you," the coach said, patting my shoulder. "There are a lot of squiggly things in the lake, but none of them will hurt you. Do you trust me enough to believe that?"

My head nodded yes, but my brain was screaming a loud *no*.

"Good. Let's give it a shot."

She started by making me put my face under the water. At first I kept my eyes squeezed shut, but then I figured I needed to see what was about to grab me, so I opened them. The weeds waving in the current on the bottom looked harmless enough. I raised up to sputter, "That wasn't too bad."

"That's the ticket," she said, now leading me to a wooden platform that stuck out into the water. "I want you to slide in feet first. This part of the lake is so shallow that it won't even be over your head."

That was probably true, but as I peered down into the water I was certain I saw something with bug eyes and tentacles staring back at me.

"Do it," Coach Barker said, her tone picking up steel.

I did. But as soon as I got in the water, I thought I felt something slithering up my leg. Panic exploded in my brain, blocking out everything but the need to get back on dry land. I thrashed, kicked, waved my arms frantically. I would have screamed, too, only my mouth was full of water.

Just when I was positive I wasn't going to make it, Coach Barker was beside me. "You're doing fine," she soothed, guiding me until my feet touched bottom.

When I straightened up my body, the water was right below my chin.

"I told you it would be okay. I suspect you've already got most of the skills you need to be a good swimmer—all you need now is to relax, practice, and believe in yourself," she assured me. "Climb back up on the pier and try again. I'll be down here waiting for you."

The next ten minutes gave a whole new meaning to the phrase "go jump in the lake." I must've done it a hundred times—okay, maybe only twenty—but it felt like a lot more. Toward the end, it was getting a tiny bit easier; I remembered how to float and I managed to coordinate my arms and legs well enough to move through the water. But the terror was still there, waiting to pounce every time Coach Barker got more than a few feet away from me.

"That's enough for today," she said after what seemed to be forever. "You've made terrific progress, Shanon. Keep it up and you'll ace the swimming test."

As I climbed huffing and puffing back up on the wooden pier, she executed a neat flip and with smooth, strong strokes headed out into the deep water.

"I'll never in life be able to do that," I mumbled to myself, plopping cross-legged on the boards. The sun felt good, and since I wasn't particularly anxious to go back and face the war again, I sat there basking and checking out the landscape.

About fifty yards away, a boy and girl were sitting on another pier that jutted out into the lake. They were alone, and as I watched, she draped her arm around his neck and snuggled against his chest. So much for Amy's no-speaking rule, I thought with an inward giggle. But my good humor soured fast when I recognized the couple: Right before my horrified eyes, Reid Olivier was making a move on Rob Williams!

Anger did weird things to me. I scrambled to my feet, determined to break up their little game. It would've taken at least five minutes for me to run around the irregular shore line, and I didn't have that much time—she was all over him, and from the looks of it, she was going to plant a kiss on him any second. My only other option was a shortcut across the water.

"I can do this," I told myself. "I'm not going to let fear stop me this time." I wouldn't be risking my life, because

I knew how to swim. And if I could just keep my mind focused on saving Lisa's relationship with Rob, I wouldn't have time to think about wriggly things in the water.

I dove in (sort of) and then chugged along, doing an awkward dog paddle until the early lessons my dad had given me kicked in. My legs started to scissor, my arms stopped splashing, and pretty soon I was managing a fairly respectable breaststroke.

About halfway to my destination, the realization that I didn't have a workable plan slowed me down a bit. If I charged up to Reid and accused her of stealing Lisa's boyfriend, she'd probably shove me back in the lake. And what would I do if Rob told me to mind my own business?

I lifted my head to glance at the pier: Rob and Reid weren't there anymore. I'd gone to all this trouble for nothing!

Without a goal to keep me going, I could no longer ignore the fact that I was all alone smack dab in the middle of a gazillion gallons of water. I was certain I'd never make it to their pier, just as sure I couldn't go back to mine. And I wasn't going to let myself sink down along the slithery fiends that were waiting at the bottom of Lake Emerald! I treaded water like crazy, praying that whatever gobbled me up would kill me with the first bite so I wouldn't suffer too much.

After a few minutes with nothing nibbling at my toes, a faint ray of hope began to dawn. Maybe the lake monsters were on a coffee break. Better still, maybe they didn't even exist.

"Shanon!" Coach Barker's shout came to me. "Don't panic—I'm on my way!"

When she reached me, I was bobbing along like a cork, still scared, but alive and kicking.

"Lie back and try to let your body float. I'm going to tow you to shore," she told me.

"I think I can make it by myself."

Kick, stroke, breathe, kick, stroke, breathe. As I followed the rhythm of the instructions in my head I felt a surge of pure delight. I was actually swimming!

Nobody would ever call me chicken again, but best of all Mars Martinez would be very proud of me.

TIME CAPSULE
ENTRY TEN:
BY PALMER DURAND

Dear Whoever Reads This in the Future,

I need someone to listen to my thoughts and problems. Since I don't have a pen pal anymore (Rain Blackburn seems to have disappeared off the face of the earth), I guess you'll have to take up the slack.

The "no-boys" rule has two main advantages. One, it doesn't matter now that none of the Ardies are interested in me because I'm not supposed to be speaking to them anyway. And two, it gives me the perfect excuse to avoid Holbrook Wellington.

Having him as my personal slave got old real quick. A couple of days after I met him I found out I didn't really have to flirt to get him to do things for me—all I had to do was ask. Where's the challenge in that? Plus, every time I turn around he's right behind me. But the worst part is that using him to do my dirty work gives me a creepy feeling. Am I actually developing a conscience?

I'd like to hash out my new ethics with the other three Foxes, but they're too busy. Since Shanon's getting over her fear of swimming, she practically lives in the water.

Maxie's still crazy over Paul, and I'm pretty sure she's been sneaking out to meet him in spite of the ban on boys. If Amy suspected, she'd blow a fuse!

The battle of the sexes is really weirding out my room-mate. She tells everybody that Nikos Smith is a macho jerk, and that she's glad they broke up. But if that's true, why does she stare at his picture when she thinks no one is watching?

She's right about one thing, though—all in all, boys are a lot more trouble than they're worth!

> *Sincerely,*
> *Palmer Durand*

With a few of my more pressing secrets off my chest, I stashed my notebook under the mattress on my bunk. My writing had gotten kind of personal lately, so I wasn't particularly anxious to have anyone else read it.

As usual, I was alone in the cabin. Reid was out keeping tabs on Rob—it seemed like all she thought about now was sneaking off to hunt for him. I regretted ever fixing them up.

"I'm bored, *bored*, BORED with this place!" I said aloud, just to hear the sound of a voice. The silence in the room was beginning to get to me.

"You wouldn't be bored if you participated in more of the camp activities," Georgette said from the doorway. She bounced in beaming, with Renee right at her heels.

"Do you always sneak up on people?" I asked, annoyed because she'd caught me talking to myself. Scanning the paint-smeared front of her T-shirt, I added an irritated, "You're an absolute mess! Where have you been?"

My tone didn't seem to faze my bubbly stepsister one bit. "At a printing session. First I carved a design on a block of wood, then I spread ink on it with a roller and pressed a sheet of paper on top."

"Spare me the details."

"Show her the print you made, Georgette," Renee urged.

A strange look crossed my stepsister's face. "She wouldn't be interested. Besides, it's not very good."

"Don't be so modest," Renee protested. "The art counselor says you have a wonderful eye for composition."

So what else was new? Georgette was brilliant at everything, and she never missed a chance to point that out to me. Why was she being so coy about showing off her talent now? It made me very suspicious. "Let's see it," I said.

Georgette hesitated for a minute, then reluctantly opened the small portfolio she was carrying.

"That's really cute." I handed it back, zapped by a familiar twinge of jealousy. I couldn't draw a straight line.

She obviously misread my sour expression. "You're upset because I used Sam's initials in the design, aren't you?"

"I've told you at least a hundred times I'm not interested in him. I wouldn't care if you tattooed his initials on your arm!" I answered with a snort.

Georgette's worried face relaxed. "I'll do a woodblock for you so you can print your own personal note cards."

"Thanks. That would be neat." Though I was touched by her offer, it made me uneasy. Why was she being so nice to me lately?

"Our group has been moved up on the Talent Night rehearsal schedule," Renee reminded us, glancing at her watch. "Where's Reid?"

I shrugged. "I guess she got hung up."

Georgette's jaw tightened with disapproval. "If she doesn't want to be in our act, she should just come right out and say so. It's very rude of her to keep us waiting."

"What difference does it make? Since we haven't decided which Greek myth we're going to use for our skit, we don't even have an act to rehearse," I pointed out.

"Reid will probably meet us at the amphitheater," Renee said. "Let's go—we've got a lot of work to do."

"You guys start walking. I'd better change my shirt," Georgette said, hanging back. Later, when she caught up with us, she handed me my hip pack. "I thought you might need this."

I eyed her warily. Her expression was all innocence, so I strapped the pouch around my waist with a careless "Thanks."

As Renee had predicted, Reid was waiting at the amphitheater, an outdoor stage ringed by tiers of wooden bleachers. From the expression on her face, I could tell that her secret meeting with Rob hadn't gone too well.

"Since you're all late, I've already started working on the script for the skit," Reid informed us huffily. "It's based on the story of Pandora's box."

Renee stiffened. "I've already blocked out a few scenes about Icarus' flight to the sun."

To head off a potential leadership problem, I decided to take control. "Both of those myths are boring. I say we do—"

"King Midas and the Golden Touch," Georgette cut in. "That's my favorite fable. Remember the guy who wished that everything he touched would turn to gold?"

"Mine, too," I said, surprised that for once we agreed on

91

something. "Dad used to read it to me when I was a little kid."

She giggled. "Didn't you love the part where he pretended to eat golden pork chops?"

"That was the best! And it used to crack me up when he . . ." I stopped, hit by a fresh wave of jealousy. My father had developed that act just for me, and I didn't appreciate my stepsister horning in on it.

I was about to say so when Renee piped up, "Since both of you vote for Midas, I guess that's what we'll do."

"There are five of us and only four parts," Reid objected. "Rob Williams will play the king, of course, and I'll be his wife. That just leaves the daughter Marigold and the messenger from the gods—"

"How did Rob get in this act?" Georgette interrupted.

"I invited him. He hasn't said yes, yet, but he will if I keep working on him," Reid told her smugly.

"Let's put the casting on hold until we finish the script," Renee suggested. "A few extra characters would punch up the Midas plot. Maybe we could add some lines for the cat to say before the king turns her into gold."

Reid's mouth twisted into a sneer. "That's tired—cats have been done to death."

"You could write in a gorilla instead," a boy's voice interjected, breaking the girl-boy speaking ban. Holbrook moved down the aisle behind us, his side-to-side shuffle a comical imitation of the animal. "I'd be perfect for the part."

Georgette and Renee giggled and even I thought it was pretty funny.

"This is a private session, Holbrook," Reid said. "You weren't invited."

The injured look in his eyes made me squirm. To my surprise, I found myself sticking up for him. "The gorilla bit might work."

"I say we do it," Georgette agreed.

Renee crossed her arms over her chest and slid Reid a cool glance. "The majority rules—Holbrook is part of the cast."

"Do you really mean it?" He looked hopeful and apprehensive at the same time. "No one ever includes me in stuff."

"We already said you're in," I told him firmly. "But since we're not supposed to speak to boys until after the challenge softball game, you can't help us write the skit."

"That's okay—I'll go work on my costume and practice my monkey walk," he responded. He was positively glowing with happiness as he scratched his sides and clumped away.

"He's such a nerd," Reid muttered.

"He's got a nice smile," I said, telling myself silently that if Holbrook would ditch his dweeby wardrobe, he might be kind of cute.

"Any girl who would even think twice about Wellington has to be terribly hard up," Reid said with a scornful laugh.

I cringed as the shot hit home.

For a minute I thought I saw worry on Georgette's face, then she started to blink spastically. "Do you have an extra tissue, Palmer? I've got something in my eye."

I unzipped my waist pouch, and as I tried to pull out a tissue, an envelope fell to the floor of the stage. "Where'd this come from?" I asked, stooping to pick up the letter.

Georgette beat me to it. "This looks like a boy's handwriting. It's addressed to you, Palmer!" she squealed, handing over the envelope.

Trying hard to hold down my excitement, I ripped it open and pulled out a note.

Dearest Palmer,

You're much too wonderful for an ordinary guy like me, so I won't try to meet you in person. I'm content to worship you from afar, though, because just the fact that we're on the same planet makes me happy. You remind me of a poem I once read. It begins, "There is a garden in her face, where roses and white lilies grow . . ." Thank you for filling all my dreams with beauty.

Forever yours,
N.S.

Renee let out a long whistle, her eyes nearly bugging from her head. "That's a seriously hot letter! Who is N.S.?"

"I think I know who it is," Reid answered.

"You do?"

"Palmer," Reid said, "isn't it obvious? N.S. stands for Nikos Smith. It's too romantic. He pretends to be interested in Amy so he can be near her roommate."

The scenario was farfetched, but at least possible. Though the memory of Nikos brushing me off popped into my mind, I ignored it. "Maybe he's just too shy to face me and tell me how he feels," I said. The possibilities of this latest development were suddenly endless: I pictured myself going to Ardsley's Homecoming Dance with the captain of the football squad!

"Let me see that," Georgette said, reaching for the note. "Well, I think the last initial is an 'F,' not an 'S.' See how the top of the letter curves?"

Renee peered over her shoulder. "It's kind of hard to tell with script. Could be either one."

Georgette nodded. "Plus, he must've smudged the ink when he was signing the note. I'm sure that's an 'F,' though."

"I can't think of any N.F. here at camp," I said, taking back my letter.

"Neither can I," Reid agreed. "It *must* be Nikos. What are you going to do about this, Palmer?"

I considered the question carefully. "Well, I know how to find out. I'll ask him to be in our Midas skit. After a couple of rehearsals, I'm sure he'll get over his shyness."

"You can't do that. It's disloyal to Amy," Georgette protested. "Come on, Renee," she said, "let's check the list of campers on the bulletin board to see if we can find an N.F." Forgetting about our skit, Georgette and Renee went off to investigate.

"She's getting weirder every day," I said.

"I'm glad they're gone. I'm dying for a smoke, aren't you?" Reid said, reaching into her pocket.

At that moment, the last thing on earth I wanted was a cigarette. I just hadn't gotten around to telling Reid I hated the things. "It's too risky right now," I said. "Nobody's seen us so far, but let's not push our luck."

"You aren't turning chicken on me, are you?"

"Of course not," I snapped indignantly. I waved toward a clump of trees behind the stage, finishing, "But we'd better go over there where we'll have some privacy."

Five minutes and three puffs later, I was ready to move

on to a more interesting activity, but Reid pulled another cigarette from her pack.

"Palmer Durand, what on earth do you think you're doing?" Shanon's voice demanded from behind us. She marched through the trees toward us carrying her camcorder, her jaw tight with anger.

I scrambled to my feet, ditching the butt I was holding. "You didn't videotape us, did you?" I asked guiltily.

"I didn't intend to, but you just happened to be in the way." She pointed to a slither of motion on the ground, adding, "I was following that cute little garter snake."

"Eeoooo yuk!" I flattened myself against the trunk of a tree. Reptiles weren't my favorite creatures.

"You little sneak—you've been spying on me all along," Reid snarled, clenching her hands into fists. "If you think you can blackmail me with that tape, you've made a big mistake!"

"Chill out, Reid. She wouldn't show the tape to anybody." Uncertainty made me ask, "Would you, Shanon?"

Without answering, she stared me down, her eyes filled with disgust.

"She won't get the chance to because she's going to give it to me right now," Reid growled, moving in.

"If you touch this camera, so help me I'll deck you," Shanon warned.

A sudden "woof" from the bushes stopped the confrontation. Gracie, the Griffiths' terrier, bounded out to run circles around us.

"What's going on, girls?" Maggie Grayson-Griffith asked as she joined the group. The stern set of her face told me there was big trouble ahead.

Shanon studied me through narrowed eyes, then

dropped her gaze. "We were just having a—a disagreement."

Relief shot through me. Reid and I owed Shanon big time for not telling on us.

"I can see that." Maggie stooped gingerly to retrieve the package of cigarettes I'd dropped on the ground. "I can also see that someone's been breaking one of Camp Emerald's strictest rules. Which one of you belongs to these?"

"I'd sooner put a lighted stick of dynamite in my mouth," Shanon declared, backing away.

I kept waiting for Reid to own up, but she just stood staring at me. My two choices—either to rat on my friend or take the rap for her—were both unacceptable. I was scouring my brain for another one when Holbrook came to the rescue.

"Those are my cigarettes," he lied, holding out his hand with a shaky, "May I please have them, Ms. Grayson-Griffith?"

Shanon gaped, but his frown warned her to silence.

Maggie glanced from me to him and back again. "Do you have anything to say about that, Palmer?"

My new code of ethics didn't include throwing myself on a live grenade. I shook my head.

Maggie looked disappointed, but she didn't challenge me. "Perhaps you're not aware of the penalty for bringing cigarettes into camp, young man. Do you realize you could be put on restriction for the rest of the session?" she asked.

He lifted his head, meeting her eyes steadily. "Yes, ma'am. I'll report to the administration center at once."

Maggie, Shanon, and Holbrook left—leaving me with Reid. "You shouldn't have let him take the rap for you," I said.

"And you," Reid added. "Really, Palmer, what's the difference between that and letting him clean up for you? Using is using."

"That's very deep, Reid," I said sarcastically. The problem was, for once, I knew Reid Olivier was right.

TIME CAPSULE
ENTRY ELEVEN:
BY MAXIE SCHLOSS

Dear Maxie,

If you want to know the truth, I think this war is plain dumb. Yeah, boys are different from girls (I'm really glad about that!) but that doesn't mean we're any better—or worse—than you all are. I'm not playing for the Oinkers because I think the game is a big mistake: The winners will gloat and the losers will mope. And even if it ends in a tie, both sides will just keep on trying to prove they're right.

All that isn't really what I wanted to tell you, but I needed to get it off my mind. Now for the good stuff. This afternoon I went to the camp photography studio and developed the pictures I took at Thaddeus's hangout. There's something very weird about them. It's hard for me to explain it without sounding crazy. You have to see for yourself. Please meet me tomorrow morning after breakfast in the woods behind the mess hall—this is serious business!

Love,
Paul

P.S. If you decide not to come because of Amy's ban on boys, I'll understand. One of the things I like best about you is your loyalty to your friends.

P.P.S. Maybe if we got together, we could figure out a way to stop the war.

At the Schloss household, going back on your word was right at the top of the no-no list. So in spite of the fact that not speaking to Paul was driving me around the bend, I was doing pretty well at keeping my promise to Amy. But when I found the note tucked in my swim bag, life got very complicated.

Amy had always been there for me when I needed help; I'd be a lousy friend not to support her now. But on the other hand, she was going overboard. Wasn't it my duty to try to stop her before she got hurt? Plus, I simply had to find out what was in those pictures. It wouldn't be as if I were sneaking out to see Paul just because I missed him— this was a real emergency.

The argument I had with myself seesawed back and forth all night, and when breakfast time rolled around, it was still a toss-up.

I was still thinking about all this, and poking holes in the stack of pancakes on my plate, when Amy sat down next to me. "You'd better finish all your food and go back for seconds," she said, frowning. "The game is tomorrow and I want all of my players to have plenty of energy."

"We don't need energy, we need a miracle," Palmer sighed, pushing her tray aside.

Shanon chimed in, "And another first baseman. I'll never be any good at that position."

"First base-*person*," Amy corrected. "If you don't think you can handle it, I'll move you to the outfield."

"You already tried that," Shanon reminded her glumly. "Yesterday I dropped three easy pop-ups and almost got beaned by a fly ball."

Amy pushed back a strand of black hair impatiently. "You'll just have to work harder at practice today."

"Amy," I said, "I think you're starting to go over the edge. You've been pushing us nonstop, and for what? No matter how well we play, we're still going to lose."

"Only if you keep thinking that way."

"Not just the girls. I mean everybody in camp is going to lose. Before you know it, our three weeks here will be over, and all we'll have to remember is a big hassle. Paul says . . ." I swallowed the rest of the sentence, but it was already too late.

"Paul?" Amy looked at me as if I'd just sold government secrets to the enemy. "Have you been sneaking out to meet Paul?"

"No, but he did write me a letter," I confessed.

"It's the same thing. The no-speaking rule means no communication of any kind between boys and girls," she reminded me.

"But that's not going to solve anything. Ignoring the problem won't settle it. If you and Nikos would just talk to each other—"

"I wouldn't speak to that creep if we were the last two people on earth," Amy snapped, jumping to her feet. "I can't believe you're acting this way, Maxie—I was sure you wouldn't let me down."

"I haven't, but you're being totally unreasonable," I protested. "Even if Paul were one of the Oinkers—which he

101

isn't—it's not fair for you to tell me I can't speak to him."

"I don't care what you do. And I also don't need you and your negative attitude on my softball team!" With that, Amy spun on her heel and stalked from the dining hall.

"She didn't mean that, Max," Shanon said, rising to her feet. "I'll go try to cool her down."

"I wish Amy had fired *me* from the team," Palmer sighed as Shanon hurried away. "It's going to be totally embarrassing when the Oinkers wipe us out."

I shot her an exasperated glance. "If you feel that way, why don't you just quit?"

She propped her elbows on the table and rested her chin on her hands. "Because I don't have anything better to do"—some of the gloom in her eyes was replaced by a sly gleam as she finished—"just yet. But that could change any day now."

Obviously, Palmer was hatching another scheme, but at the moment, I didn't have time to figure it out. The only good thing was that I was officially off the hook now, so I could meet Paul without feeling guilty.

As promised, he was waiting for me behind the mess hall. "You look really down," he said. "What's wrong?"

"Nothing major." There was no point dragging him into my disagreement with Amy, so I changed the subject. "What's the big deal about the pictures?"

Without explaining, he handed me two eight-by-ten enlargements.

"Yuk—I had my eyes closed, and my hair is a mess," I said, rating my own image, "but you look terrific."

"Forget about us and check out the house."

I saw nothing out of the ordinary until he pointed to a

window on the ground floor. It was vacant in the photo of me standing alone in front of the Blackthorn house, but in the picture of me and Paul together, there was a dark, blurry form behind the paneless frame!

A sudden, icy electricity raised the hairs on the nape of my neck. "That couldn't be a ghost, could it?"

"I don't know what it is, but I'd like to find out. One of the counselors showed me an overland shortcut to the place. We could be there in less than twenty minutes."

I'd always thought it was really dumb for movie characters to go bopping off to a house they suspected was haunted. Now I was holding fairly convincing proof that something weird was going on in old Thaddeus's hangout. Plus, I was due in crafts class in five minutes, and if I cut I'd be risking demerits. But none of that stopped me from saying, "Let's do it. As future scientists, it's our duty to investigate."

The shortcut to the Blackthorn house was even more spooky than the route we'd taken before. It didn't help any that the sky had turned gray and heavy. This time we approached the house from the opposite direction. When the back of the stone building reared up in the heart of the dense pine forest, a shiver of dread stopped me in my tracks. "Are we sure we want to do this?" I quavered.

Paul swallowed hard and took a quarter from his pocket. "Heads we explore, tails we get the heck out of here."

The coin came down from his flip, wobbled on the hard-packed ground, and finally settled on the tails side.

It was crazy to ignore such an obvious warning, but I heard myself saying, "It's kind of a waste to come all this way for nothing."

Paul reached for my hand. I clasped his fingers tightly,

and as we walked toward the house, I could almost hear eerie music rising in the background. The rear door was jammed shut, but there was an open window set high in the wall beside it.

"I'll go first and let you in," he said, shoving an old rain barrel against the house. Before I could object, he'd climbed up on it and was wriggling through the opening.

While I waited, shifting uneasily from foot to foot, the wind moaned through the branches of the trees. It was definitely spooky. I called out a nervous, "Speed it up, will you?" at the same instant the door creaked open.

I stepped into what had to have been the kitchen; there were warped cabinets lining one wall and a tin sink under the window. The room was otherwise empty except for a rusty range in one corner.

"I saw a stove like that in a museum. It burns wood," Paul said, studying it curiously.

"Imagine having to chop down a tree just to scramble an egg! I bet Thad's daughter would have paid big bucks for a microwave."

Paul chuckled, but it was definitely a nervous chuckle. The door that led to the rest of the first floor was blocked from the other side; although we shoved with all our might, it wouldn't budge.

"We can go around to the front and explore the living room later. Let's see what's on the second story," Paul suggested, leading the way to the stairs at the far side of the kitchen.

The stairwell had no windows, but there was enough daylight coming from somewhere above to let us see where we were going. Paul tested each step on the way up. The narrow boards groaned ominously underfoot, but they were sturdy enough to hold our weight. Just past the top landing, a hallway extended along the width of the building; at the end was another flight of stairs that apparently descended into the living room.

The second level of the house was a mess—half the floorboards had been ripped up, and huge holes were gouged out of the plaster walls. Most of the ceiling was gone, and I could see the sky through the rafters overhead.

"Who could have totaled the place?" I wondered aloud.

"Looters. Thaddeus was supposed to have stashed a load of gold somewhere in this house, and after he hanged himself, a bunch of men from a village down the road came looking for it."

"How did you know that?"

"I found a book about the old legends of this area in the camp library," Paul explained. "It said the treasure was never found, and when weird things started happening here, people were too scared to keep looking."

"I know the feeling," I mumbled, now having serious second thoughts about this adventure. "What kind of weird things?"

"Mysterious lights in the windows at night, strange noises—standard ghost stuff. The story goes that one of the kids from the village saw a—"

His rundown was interrupted by a scrabbling, scratchy noise from behind. Every nerve in my body went on red alert, and when I spun around, I was looking at a huge, fluffy squirrel. After a stream of irritated chirps, the squirrel gave us a flip of his fuzzy tail and dove into one of the holes in the floor.

"My hair is going to be completely gray by the time we get out of here," I gulped.

"*If* we get out," Paul teased as he pushed open a door to the right of the corridor.

Surprisingly, the room beyond hadn't been trashed. There were even a few pieces of furniture left—the remains of a four-poster bed, a small dresser with its drawers missing, and a cracked mirror attached to the door of a closet.

"This must've been Charity Blackthorn's bedroom," I guessed, running my fingers over a patch of rose-patterned paper that still clung to the wall. For some reason, the atmosphere here was different from the rest of the house—more peaceful, happier even. The air even smelled different, as if it had been scented with a faint touch of flowers, and I began to relax.

Paul moved over to the window to stare out into the yard. "The night she died, she must've stood here watching the British soldiers lay an ambush for Jonathan Quiggins, her boyfriend."

I wandered to his side, now caught up in the long-ago tragedy. "What happened to him?"

"He was killed during the battle of Lexington and Concord. Afterward, he was buried in the churchyard next to Charity." Paul sent me a sidelong glance, adding, "That's another reason why old Thad haunts the place. Supposedly, there was a feud between him and the Quiggins family. People speculated that even after death, he hated the thought of his daughter being near Jonathan."

"It's like *Romeo and Juliet*." I sighed. "Parents can really screw up your social life."

"Lucky for us, we don't have that problem." Paul slipped his arm around my waist. "When I called home last night to wish Dad happy birthday, I found out he's a Maximilian Schloss fan. He met your father at a charity benefit that was sponsored by the automobile company."

"Wonderful," I groaned. From the twinkle in Paul's eyes, I could tell there was more to the story. Steeling myself for the worst, I pleaded, "Don't tell me my father sprayed yours with canned whipped cream."

"Nope—they smooshed lemon pies in each other's faces. Dad loved it, and after the show they went to dinner together." His arm tightened around me and he smiled. "Like father, like daughter. Remember when you squirted me with seltzer at the Halloween party?"

"You'll never let me forget that, will you?"

He caught my hand, smiling as he pulled me closer. I was positive he was going to kiss me again, so I closed my eyes.

And heard a loud series of what I can only describe as dragging thumps coming from the first floor. Paul and I froze, still clinging to each other, but now because of fear instead of hormones.

"That's probably another squirrel," he whispered.

"If it is, he must weigh a ton!" Beads of sweat popped out on my forehead—which was weird, because I was freezing. The bumping got louder, and along with it came the same grunting, groaning howl we'd heard the day of our picnic, only it was more awesome this time because it was a lot closer.

I was now too terrified to breathe, much less speak. Luckily, my legs were still in working order. I clutched Paul's arm, practically dragging him along in my haste to make a getaway. Panic had blanked a lot of important things from my brain—like the missing boards out in the corridor. Two steps past Charity's door, I skidded into a hole and my foot got stuck between two floor joists. Paul knelt down and began pulling on my leg, and the noise on the first story changed directions. It now seemed to be moving in the vicinity of the stairs that led up from the living room.

"I think it's coming up here," Paul whispered.

Sure enough, there was a *lumpity-thump-thump* hitting the treads of the steps.

I tugged at my foot so hard that a pain shot through my ankle, but it wouldn't budge. "See if you can untie my shoelace," I gasped, peering over my shoulder at the landing. Any second now, I expected to see a ghastly, transparent version of Thaddeus Blackthorn's corpse.

Paul gave up on the knot and broke the lace with a frantic jerk. "Got it!"

My foot slipped out of my high-top sneaker at the exact same instant as the mysterious resident of Thaddeus Blackthorn's house appeared at the top of the landing. For the space of a heartbeat, we all were frozen, then I screamed and Paul yelled. The brown bear cub let out a scared howl and scooted back down the stairs.

"Mama and Papa Bear are probably playing bridge in the living room—let's get the heck out of here," Paul squawked.

I'd invested a month's allowance in my pink Reeboks, but I left the one in the floor behind without a second thought. Hand in hand, Paul and I pelted along the hallway and down the rear stairs. We didn't slow down until the house was well out of sight.

When the humor of the situation hit me, I stopped short, caught up in a fit of helpless laughter. "Did you check out the expression on Baby Bear's face?" I gasped, wiping tears from my eyes. "I'll bet he was twice as scared as we were."

Paul leaned against me, hiccuping with hilarity. "I don't think so. For a while there, I thought I was having a heart attack."

"This is going to be one of our all-time great stories."

His arms tightened around me. "Let's not tell anyone. That way, Thaddeus Blackthorn and the brown bear will always be our own special secret."

TIME CAPSULE ENTRY TWELVE: BY AMY HO

The morning of the softball game dawned chilly and gray, with a brisk breeze blowing. I stared at the heavy sky through the cabin window, feeling nearly as dismal as the weather. My troops were deserting left and right. The roster of thirty girls who'd signed up for my team was down to a measly ten—most of them complete rookies who hardly knew which end of the bat to hit with.

Not only that, peace was breaking out all over! During the first few days of the war, couples had been scarce in camp. Now it was business as usual—boys and girls strolling across the quad, eating together in the mess hall—I could hardly believe how little my sisters-at-arms cared about the way the guys had dumped on us.

But the worst part was that Amy Ho, fearless crusader for female equality, was as sick of the battle as everyone else. Pride and anger at Nikos Smith were the only things that kept me going.

I turned away from the window to find an obvious lack of team spirit in the cabin. Shanon was writing another letter to Mars, and the King Midas crew was tied up with their skit.

"You can't be the daughter, Georgette. You're too . . . uh . . . short," Palmer snapped.

"I'm not short, I'm petite," Georgette objected, "and I'm perfect for the part of Marigold. Every time Dad read me the story, he'd say I was his golden girl."

Palmer scowled. "That's what he used to call me!"

"Why don't we change the story so Midas has two daughters?" Renee suggested diplomatically.

As far as I was concerned, my team had enough problems without the Durands fighting each other. "I'm going to sing my anti-boy song at Talent Night," I broke into the conversation. "My big finale is a new verse about the Foxy Feminist Forces wiping out the Oinkers."

"It'll be a miracle if F.F.F. scores one run," Reid scoffed.

I'd disliked Reid from the word go, but now I was working on a real hate. Ignoring her, I turned to Palmer. "Since Jennifer's out of the lineup, you get to be my starting catcher."

Palmer avoided my gaze. "I can't play this afternoon. When we finish the script, I've got to start on my costume."

Perfect. Another desertion. Still, I wasn't about to beg anyone to play for me. "Suit yourself," I said with what I hoped was a casual shrug. "Georgette's a better catcher anyway."

Georgette squirmed. "I'm a really lousy athlete, Amy. The team would be better off without me."

"I'm not all that great, and I'm going to play," Shanon piped up loyally from the other side of the room.

"Me, too," Renee joined in.

Georgette's mouth became a stubborn line. "I'm not going to go out on that diamond and make a fool of myself."

"If you drop out, I won't have enough players to field a team!"

Maxie hurried into the cabin in time to catch the tail end of the discussion. "Don't sweat it, because the game's sure to be called off. There's a storm moving in from the west."

"Says who?" I snapped. Things had been tense between us since our argument the other day.

"When I was at the rec center watching TV, the weatherman cut in with a forecast of rain, hail, and gale-force winds," she answered coolly. "Everyone's supposed to meet at the mess hall in fifteen minutes—we've all got to help secure the camp."

"Is it really that serious?" Shanon asked.

Maxie nodded. "One of the counselors said this area was hit by a big storm summer before last. The road into camp was blocked by fallen trees and the power was off for three days."

The report had hardly gotten past her lips when the rest of the gang headed for the door. I was about to follow when Maxie grabbed my arm. "I'll be on your team if there's a game today."

I knew that I'd been out of line when I blew up at her, but stubbornness kept me from saying so. "Don't do me any favors. You still think the game is a mistake, don't you?"

"Yeah, but that won't keep me from playing to win."

We stood eyeball to eyeball, and I was the first to blink. "Thanks, Maxie. I'm sorry I've been so snotty."

"Forget it." Grinning, she gave my shoulder an encour-

112

aging pat. "Who knows—if we do win, Nikos may change his mind about girls being weak, and the two of you can get together again."

"I wouldn't take that creep back if he came crawling on his hands and knees," I lied, trailing her through the door.

Outside, the clouds spilling over the western horizon looked like mountains of dirty soap suds. As I ducked my head against the stiffening wind, it occurred to me that "stormy" was the perfect adjective for my relationship with Nikos: Whenever we got together, there was bound to be thunder and lightning.

I was so caught up in the idea that I didn't notice another camper cutting across my path. We ran into each other with a thump that sent me sprawling.

"Sorry," Nikos muttered, extending his hand to help me up.

My fingers almost touched his before I remembered how mad I was and snatched them back. I scrambled to my feet with a frosty, "You should watch where you're going."

His jaw tightened. "It was an accident. I said I was sorry."

I gave him my best withering glance, then turned away. "Wait up—can we talk?" he asked, grasping my arm.

I shook off his hand. "I have nothing to say to a person who'd pull a stupid panty raid."

"I didn't do that," he protested. "And while we're on the subject of dirty tricks, I didn't short-sheet the beds in your cabin or put up the sign in the mess hall, either."

"Oh, yeah?" The sincerity in his eyes threw me for a second, but I followed up with, "Well, you're the leader of the Oinkers, so technically you're responsible for everything they do."

113

Nikos threw up his hands in disgust. "It's impossible to talk to girls," he said to nobody in particular.

"If you make one more chauvinistic remark, I'm going to—"

"You two put a cork in it," Mr. Griffith said sternly, stepping between us. "Maggie's down by the lake directing the crew that's securing the equipment. Go give her a hand."

"This morning at breakfast, she looked a little tired. Shouldn't she be resting?" I asked.

The concern in his eyes deepened. "Yes, but she insists on doing her share."

"Don't worry, I'll watch out for her," Nikos told him.

I was tempted to say it would probably be the other way around, but thought better of it. "Me, too," I piped up.

"I'm counting on you both," Mr. G. said, hurrying away.

Nikos and I walked to the lakefront keeping a careful distance between us; each time he lengthened his stride I matched him, determined not to let him outdo me at anything. But then I stole a sidewise look at him, and what I saw wasn't what I'd expected. Nikos looked hurt and angry and confused. He looked exactly the way I felt. *Maybe he'd told the truth when he said he hadn't played the practical jokes,* I thought miserably. *And maybe I'd been wrong to be so mean to him.* I was about to say I was sorry when he glanced over and caught me studying him.

A dark flush rose in his face and his eyes turned cold. "What are you looking at?" he demanded.

So much for an apology—the war was on again. "Not

much," I snapped back, taking off at a swift jog as I spotted Maggie.

Nikos got to her a beat ahead of me. "Just point me to a job, Mrs. G.-G., and it's as good as done."

I stepped in front of him. "Dan sent *me* to help you."

"There's enough work to go around," she said. "Nikos, you help the guys tie up the canoes. Amy, you latch the shutters on the boat house. I'm going to—"

"Find a comfortable spot and park," I finished, looking pointedly at the mound covered by her oversize blouse. "I'm sure little Osgood or Wilhelmina could use a break."

"This baby's going to have more names than the Crown Prince of England," Maggie said, laughing. As a gust of wind swirled her hair, her expression turned serious. "Get to work, guys—I suspect we don't have much time left before the storm hits."

There was an ominous growl of thunder as I hurried down the path along the shore, and I glanced up at a bank of clouds that seemed twice as dark as it had been ten minutes ago.

I latched the two front windows on the boat house in nothing flat. *I'll be finished with my chore long before Nikos*, I gloated to myself. But the window in back was a different story. The prop that held the overhanging shutter open apparently hadn't been pulled out for some time, and it was hard to move. The other problem was a brownish-gray object that looked like a lopsided Japanese lantern. The papery lump was the size of a basketball, and it was suspended from the underside of the shutter.

Though it didn't appear to be solid enough to keep the

115

shutter from closing, I decided to get rid of it anyway. A dead branch I found on the ground was the perfect length; I poised it over my shoulder like a bat and took my best swing. The stick connected with a satisfying whack, and the ugly mass sailed through the air and squashed against the trunk of a nearby tree.

My first clue that something was terribly wrong was an angry buzzing. Then I turned to see where it was coming from, and I spotted a dark brown cloud pouring from the object I'd just knocked down. Being from New York, I hadn't had much experience with a bunch of ticked-off wasps, but logic said my only move was a fast getaway.

I hadn't counted on their speed, though. Before I'd gone two steps, the insects were all over me, diving in my face, tangling in my hair, even zooming under the loose tail of my T-shirt!

There must have been a zillion of those little suckers, every one of them determined to take a chunk out of me. At first I was numb with shock, then white-hot needles of pain jabbed through every inch of my body. I staggered around the corner of the boat house, screaming and swatting madly at the swarm. No matter what I did, the wasps just kept coming.

"Amy!"

I heard Maggie's horrified shout, but I couldn't see her. My eyelids were shut as tight as I could get them.

"Don't come near me," I screamed, nearly choking on my panic. Sure that I was going to die and determined not to take my teacher and her baby with me, I ran blindly in the opposite direction.

As if I weren't in enough trouble, something heavy suddenly hit me, knocking me to the ground. Before I could figure out what was happening, a thick cloth was wrapped around my head. I waved my arms feebly, hurting too badly to do much more.

"Keep still—I'm trying to help you," Nikos shouted in my ear.

He scooped me up and started to run at top speed. "Take a deep breath," he ordered. "We're going in the lake."

The shock of the cold water relieved some of the pain. I surfaced, sputtering, hanging on to Nikos for dear life, and babbling about what had happened. He wrapped his arms around me, but I couldn't stop the tears that were streaming down my face.

"It's okay—the wasps are gone now," he said, awkwardly pushing my wet hair away from my forehead.

By now, a crowd had gathered by the edge of the water. When Nikos carried me to shore, a loud cheer went up. Mr. Griffith met us near the pier.

"That was a fine piece of work, Smith," he congratulated. "I'll take Amy now."

Nikos looked kind of disappointed, but he deposited me carefully in Mr. G.'s arms.

After an hour in the infirmary, I was certain I would live, but not so sure I'd ever look human again. There were over forty stings on my face and arms, all of which had been smeared with a greasy salve. As though I hadn't been punctured enough, the doctor zapped me with an injection to prevent an allergic reaction.

"Will I have to go home because of this?" I asked anxiously as he transferred me to a narrow hospital bed.

"We're keeping you here overnight to see if complications develop, but my guess is you'll be back with your friends tomorrow," he assured me.

A few minutes after he left, Maggie came in. "How are you feeling, honey?" she asked gently.

"Like a greased pig," I said. "I must look an absolute mess."

"You're beautiful. You were also brave and unselfish to keep the wasps away from me." She leaned down and brushed my forehead with a light kiss. "Nikos thinks you're pretty special, too. He's waiting in the hall."

I immediately covered my face with my hands, groaning, "Tell him to go away—I'm too ugly!"

"I have seen you look better, but what the heck—I kind of like lumpy girls." Nikos walked into the room with a broad smile and a brown paper sack. "Since you missed lunch, I brought you a doggie bag. The doctor says it's okay if you eat."

"That reminds me—Dan's taking me into town for dinner tonight. I'd better start getting ready," Maggie said, beating a tactful retreat as Nikos dragged a chair up to my bed.

Pulling the sheet over my face, I sent him a muffled, "Thanks—I owe you one."

"It was nothing. We macho types are supposed to look after poor pea-brained girls who use wasp nests for batting practice."

I sat up and threw my pillow at him.

"Just teasing," he said, ducking. As he straightened up, his face wore a serious expression. "I was really worried when I heard you screaming. I thought you were being attacked by a bear."

"I might have come out better if I had," I said, gingerly

touching one of the many bumps on my arm. "Would you have come to the rescue if it had been a bear?"

"No question. A two-ton hair ball with teeth is no match for the great Nikos Smith!"

"Don't start with me," I warned, giggling in spite of myself. "Did you get a lot of stings?"

"Only a couple. I guess wasps like Foxes better than Oinkers." He leaned back, meeting my gaze steadily. "I've been thinking—after the storm, it'll probably take a couple of days for the field to dry out enough to play. Do you think the others would mind if we canceled the game?"

"Nope. Everybody's getting sick of softball anyway—especially me."

"Me, too. And I'm also tired of us being enemies. If it's okay with you, I'd like us to start all over again." He straightened his shoulders and plunged on, "Hi, Amy—I'm Nikos. Sometimes I say dumb things, and now and then I act like an arrogant jerk. Deep down, though, I'm not such a bad guy. I'd like to be your friend because you're funny and pretty and smart, and you don't take guff from anybody. Plus, I really want to learn to play the guitar."

When he'd finished his spiel, he stuck out his hand.

I shook it. "Hi, Nikos. I'm Amy. My temper gets out of hand sometimes, and it's very hard for me to admit that I'm wrong. I'm sorry I dumped spaghetti on you, but you did look cute with tomato sauce dripping down your face." I couldn't resist adding, "Even though I like you a lot, you're nuts to root for the Chicago Cubs."

"I'm going to overlook that—the wasp poison has obviously gone to your brain." Nikos's smile took the sting from his words, and he gave my fingers an extra squeeze before he let them go. "Now that we're through negotiating a truce, let's eat," he said, taking carry-out cartons from his bag.

Suddenly I was starving. "What's for lunch?"

Nikos's mouth widened into a grin. "Barbecued pork ribs—what else?"

TIME CAPSULE
ENTRY THIRTEEN:
BY PALMER DURAND

Dear Time Capsule Person,

You'd think Amy was a celebrity the way people fuss over her. The morning she got out of the infirmary, her favorite breakfast was served in the mess hall, and our table was decorated with a bunch of wildflowers. At first I was really worried about her, and I have to admit she's got a lot of guts. If I'd had to appear in public with my face all puffy, I would have died of embarrassment, but she just made jokes about the way she looked. Now that her swelling is going down, though, I think she should quit hogging the spotlight. What's the big deal about a few bee bites?

The romantic letter Nikos Smith sent did wonders for my morale. Wasn't I silly to think I was losing my sex appeal? Since the softball game was canceled, he's spending a lot of time with Amy again. Of course, you and I both know that's because he needs a good excuse to hang around our cabin. Amy's crazy about him—that's for sure—and when the truth comes out, it's going to be really tough on her. But it isn't fair to any of us to let her go on believing he's her boyfriend when all the time he's secretly in love with me! As soon as Nikos and I get together, we'll have to think of some way to let Amy down easy. After all, she is my roommate and I do care about her. First things first, though. Nikos is obviously shy, and my big problem is getting him to admit how he really feels about me.

I wish I could talk it over with Maxie and Shanon, but they'd accuse me of trying to steal Nikos from Amy. The last person in the world I'd ask for advice is Reid—she doesn't know squat about boys! The way she throws herself at Rob is really pathetic. Not that I have anything against chasing guys—I do it all the time. I just think it's tacky to be so obvious about it. Besides, ever since the smoking incident, I've sort of stayed away from Reid.

While we're on the subject, you'll be glad to know that Holbrook didn't get busted for taking the cigarette rap. Mrs. G.-G. went to bat for him, and the camp director let him off with a warning. I'm sure Maggie suspects that Reid and I were really to blame, but she can't accuse us without proof. Which means I've simply got to convince Shanon to erase the video she shot of Reid and me smoking!

I'm getting writer's cramp so I'll sign off for now, but I'll be sure to keep you posted on the progress of Operation N.S.

Regards and all that junk,
Palmer Durand

Stuffing my notebook back into my tote bag, I glanced at my watch. According to a conversation I'd overheard between Nikos and Amy, he was supposed to wind up his hike by 2:30. That meant he should be coming along the trail by the stream any second now.

I'd had the place staked out for the past half hour, and though waiting was a drag, I couldn't afford to pass up a chance to meet him in private. My scheme was to pretend I'd lost my way while I was wandering through the woods. Naturally, he would offer to guide me back to camp, and somewhere along the way, I'd bring up the subject of his letter. It was old stuff, but it usually worked like a charm.

Meanwhile, since I was getting hungry, I pulled a candy bar from my bag and settled down for some serious munching.

"What are you doing here, Palmer?" Nikos asked from behind.

I nearly choked on a mouthful of chocolate. And I promptly forgot all the details of my plan. I decided to wing it. "Enjoying the scenery. It's so beautiful and quiet here."

"You probably shouldn't be in these woods alone. There are lots of wild animals running around loose."

"I hadn't thought of that." I hung my head, looking properly sorry for my mistake. "I'm so glad you came by. Do you mind if I walk back to camp with you?"

He frowned, then his shoulders lifted in a shrug. "Okay, but you have to keep up. I'm supposed to watch Amy rehearse her song for Talent Night and I don't want to be late."

"What a coincidence! I have to be at the amphitheater this afternoon, too. I'm acting in a play based on the King Midas story." When that didn't produce a response, I continued, "Would you like to be in it? We'd be glad to add another character to the cast"

"Acting's not my thing," he answered, jogging off.

I matched his pace, but not without a struggle. "I have to tell you how brave you were to save Amy from those bees."

"Wasps."

"Whatever. What I meant was, it's unusual to find a talented athlete who's also unselfish and sensitive." I wanted to add handsome, but that would've been laying it on a bit thick.

Nikos angled a sharp glance my way. "Was that a shot?"

The resentment in his eyes caught me off guard. "No—I really mean it. I'll bet you're concerned about important things like world peace and acid rain, and I'm sure you like poetry."

"It's okay."

We were in sight of camp now, so I didn't have long to make a breakthrough. I turned my smile up a notch and pressed on, "My favorite poem in the whole world starts, 'There is a garden in her face, where roses and white lilies grow.'"

A blush zipped over Nikos's face. "I'm not sure what you want me to say about that, Palmer, and I don't have time to find out." He raced away from me, calling back a terse, "Check you later."

I stared after him, not sure what to think. Most of the time he had acted as though he didn't want me around. But the embarrassment on his face when I quoted the poem was a dead giveaway. After stewing for a while, I decided that he was so shy, the only way he could communicate was through letters. Sitting down beside the path, I pulled out my notebook and dashed off a note.

Dear N.S.

Your letter was really sweet. This is just to let you know that I feel the same way about you.

Your dream girl,
P.D.

I congratulated myself for keeping it simple; moving too fast would just scare him off. Now I'd have to find some subtle way to deliver the note.

When I reached the amphitheater (after a small detour to the cabin to put on more makeup) Shanon was onstage videotaping while Amy tuned her guitar. Amy waved at me, smiling, and for a minute seeing her look so happy made me distinctly uncomfortable. But my guilt wasn't strong enough to make me abandon my master plan.

Nikos was seated on a bench near the front of the amphitheater. My gaze zeroed in on the knapsack he'd been carrying; it was lying in the aisle to his right. I caught his eye, winked at him, and then went over to join the others who were in my skit.

"We've been waiting for you for ages!" Reid said, scowling as I sat down beside her.

A quick glance around told me why she was bent out of shape. Though Georgette, Renee, and Holbrook were a few rows away running lines, there was no sign of Rob Williams.

"Since Midas isn't here, you couldn't have started the rehearsal anyway," I pointed out.

On cue, Rob bounded down the aisle. "Sorry I'm late," he apologized, passing us to head for a spot next to the others.

Reid popped up to intercept him. "Come sit with me so

we can go over our first scene," she purred. "Palmer was just leaving."

I got up with a careless shrug, and Rob slumped down in my seat. I as pretty sure he wasn't thrilled about being left alone with Reid—something about the set of his shoulders reminded me of a fly caught in a spiderweb. I felt kind of sorry for him, but right then my main concern was getting closer to Nikos's knapsack.

I was halfway to the front when Shanon charged up to meet me.

"Why did you leave Reid alone with Rob?" she asked irritably.

"Chill out—they're just rehearsing."

"Yeah, but for what?" Her gaze turned accusing and bore into me. "You're the one who fixed them up, aren't you?"

"I didn't see any harm in introducing them."

"He's Lisa's boyfriend," she reminded me for the umpteenth time. "We can't just stand back and watch Reid snatch him!"

Though it was against my best interests, I reluctantly suggested, "You could use that videotape to blackmail her."

"That would be dishonest. Besides, Mr. Griffith's planning to show a collage from the tapes at Alma's first assembly next fall, and I've already erased the part with you and Reid smoking."

I was so relieved I almost hugged Shanon. "I owe you big time for that, and just for the record, I'll never touch another cigarette as long as I live."

"Good plan. Now that I've saved your lungs, I've got to go keep an eye on Reid and Rob," Shanon said, turning away.

I caught her arm. "If Rob and Reid really want to get together, you can't stop them."

"I wouldn't be very loyal to Lisa if I didn't at least try," she responded, heading up the aisle.

The conversation firmed up a few things in my own head: Amy was my friend, and it would be much better for her to face reality now than to go on believing that Nikos was crazy about her. With a clear conscience, I headed down the aisle toward the knapsack, stopping a few rows short of the target.

Amy finished her song, and everyone else who was waiting to rehearse their own acts gave her a standing ovation. Nikos went up on the stage to congratulate her.

In less than ten seconds, I'd reached the knapsack, unzipped a side pocket, delivered my mail, and strolled back up the aisle.

Georgette, now sitting alone, looked up from her script as I slipped into the seat beside her "There's a group ahead of us on the rehearsal schedule, so Renee and Holbrook went to get some sodas. I told them to bring you back a diet cola," she said, smiling. "You look happier than you have in days. What's up?"

She had been so nice to me lately that I figured she deserved to hear the details of my recent coup. Plus, I was dying to tell somebody, and she was the only person around. "You're looking at Ardsley's next homecoming queen," I said. "Since my new boyfriend will be the Lions' quarterback, I've practically got it sewn up."

Georgette's expression was total confusion. "You want to run that by me again?"

I glanced around warily. "Let's go find someplace where we can talk in private."

We sat down on a bench in the back tier of seats, and I told her the story of the rendezvous in the woods, adding a few minor details for effect.

"Please tell me you didn't go to meet Nikos because of that dumb letter," Georgette moaned.

"Why else? Now shut up and let me finish."

When I reached the mail drop part her face went ghost pale. "You shouldn't have done that, Palmer! Nikos really likes Amy."

"If he did, he wouldn't have written all of those romantic things to me."

"He didn't." She scrunched down in her seat, her next words so low I could bearly hear them. "I wrote the letter and put it in your hip pack. I knew there was no guy in camp with the initials N.F., so I used them. I tried to tell you that last letter wasn't an 'S,' but you wouldn't listen."

My temperature went through several changes before finally settling on subzero. "Why would you do a dumb thing like that?"

"Because you've been so depressed about guys lately. I didn't want you to get an inferiority complex," she explained. Her bottom lip was quivering as though she were about to cry. "I'll admit I've done some sneaky things to you, but this wasn't one of them. I was only trying to help—you've got to believe that!"

I did, but it didn't keep me from wanting to do her in. "Do you realize that you've just trashed the rest of my life? Nikos is going to think I'm the biggest dweeb on two legs. And I'll have to move out of Suite 3-D, because Amy, Shanon, and Maxie will never speak to me again. I've got to get that note back before he sees it!"

128

"If you can distract him, I'll steal his knapsack," Georgette offered.

It was a workable strategy, but it had one major flaw: By the time we got back to the front of the amphitheater, Amy, Nikos, and the knapsack were long gone.

Georgette's eyes filled with tears. "Please say you'll forgive me, Palmer. I'll find some way to get you out of this mess."

"If you don't, you'll spend the rest of your life regretting it," I promised.

TIME CAPSULE
ENTRY FOURTEEN:
BY SHANON DAVIS

Dear Shanon,

If you're not sitting down right now, do it! Then take a deep breath and hang on to your seat, 'cause I don't want this to blow you away. Okay, are you ready?????

I'M COMING BACK TO ALMA!!!

The downside is that my mother and father are definitely divorcing each other. Although it still hurts, I'm getting used to the idea. After going through the separation hassle for a whole year, I've finally decided that this way will be best for the whole family. And who knows? Maybe with some of the pressure off, Mom and Dad will learn how to be friends again. Meanwhile, I can't wait to get back to boarding school, where things are normal. You can imagine how rough it's been here if I can think of life in Suite 3-D as normal! Ha-ha!

I'm mailing Rob a letter at the same time I send yours, but just in case his arrives late, be sure to tell him the news as soon as you see him. The last few times I've heard from him, he's been a little skimpy on details of what he's doing, but then again, how much can you squeeze on the back of

130

a postcard? I'm hoping that A) he'll have time to write me a real letter soon, and B) he'll be as happy about me coming back to school as I am.

   Tell everybody I said Hi, and that I send hugs all around. Won't it be terrifically, wonderfully SUPER for the whole gang to be together again?

Love,
Lisa

P.S. As a special treat, Mom's taking me shopping next week to pick out new spreads and curtains for our room. Let me know soonest what colors and styles you're into now.

After I finished reading Lisa's letter aloud to the other Foxes, I let loose a whoop that rattled the windows of the cabin. "This is too good to be true!" I squealed, bouncing around to deliver Lisa's hugs to Amy and Palmer. When I got to Maxie, I pulled her to her feet and danced her around in a circle. "You've heard so much about Lisa that you probably already feel like you know her. But when you meet her in person, you'll love her as much as the rest of us do!"

"I'm sure she's really neat. I'm very happy for you, Shanon," Maxie said, suddenly pulling away to glance at her watch. "Oops—gotta go. The swimming meet is day after tomorrow, and Paul and I have to practice."

I stared after her as she beat a hasty retreat through the doorway. "What's with her?" I asked. "Maybe she's stressed out from spending every spare minute in the pool."

"And you call me insensitive," Palmer snorted. "I can't believe you read the part about the new spreads and drapes aloud. From the look on Maxie's face, I'd say she got the message!"

"What message?"

"It's pretty obvious that since Lisa's coming back, you're planning to dump Maxie," Amy explained.

"Lisa and I haven't even talked about rooming together again. I guess she just assumed that we would," I said, suddenly aware of how the situation must look to Maxie, and totally miserable about it. "I'm not going to dump anybody."

"You'll have to do something. There's only enough space in 3-D for four people," Palmer reminded me.

"We'll have to move into a larger suite," I said, dismayed at the thought of having to choose between my two roommates. In their own special ways, Lisa and Maxie were both my best friends.

"You're right," I said. "I'd better find Maxie."

Swimming practice hadn't started when I reached the pool. Maxie was alone doing underwater laps fast enough to win an Olympic event. Finally she came up for air. "I need to talk to you, Max," I said.

Clearly reluctant, she flipped over and backstroked to the concrete apron. Her "What's up?" was polite, but distant.

"I didn't mean—that is, I'm sorry if you thought—"

"You don't owe me an apology, Shanon," she interrupted, tossing her wet hair out of her eyes. "Lisa's very important to you. I've known from the beginning that I was only a temporary replacement. I'll just ask to be transferred to another suite—no pain, no strain."

I could tell by the hurt in her eyes that was a lie. "Please don't do that. I'm sure Maggie will help us arrange something."

"We can still hang out together sometime, no matter where I live," Maxie said carelessly. There was the merest hint of a tremble to her bottom lip as she finished, "I think that would work better for me than being a fifth wheel." Not giving me a chance to object, she pushed off and headed into another lap.

With nothing to do and a lot of time to do it in, I went back to our now-empty cabin to pick up my camcorder. Most of what I got that afternoon was background—interesting patches of lichen on the tree trunks, fat squirrels perched on branches, the wide reach of the White Mountains towering against the sky.

When I wandered into an isolated glen about a quarter mile from camp, I lucked upon a red fox. Shafts of sunshine filtering through the leaves overhead touched the animal's coat with gleaming copper—it was the exact color of Maxie's hair.

But before I could get my camcorder in position, a rustling came from the bushes to my left. The fox split the scene so fast I couldn't tell which way it had gone.

Rob Williams pushed through the underbrush and hurried to my side. "You're not on Reid Olivier's trail again, are you?" he asked, glancing around warily.

"I wouldn't waste one inch of tape on her," I snapped. "And for your information, you've just ruined the best video shot I'll ever get a chance to take in my whole life!"

Rob apologized, but the expression on his face was more anxious than sorry. "I saw you headed this way, and I followed because I need your help. I've got a serious problem with Reid."

For a second I was too stunned to speak, then I lit into him furiously. "Do I look like Ann Landers? In case it's slipped your mind, I'm Lisa McGreevy's best friend!"

"I know, and that's why—"

"Lisa depends on you. She's managing to get through this divorce thing because she thinks you're in her corner. How do you suppose she'll feel when she finds out you're fooling around with a dweeby twit like Reid Olivier?"

"I'm not fooling around."

"Well, if you're *serious* about Reid, you're in worse shape than I thought." I was so mad I was practically spitting sparks. "You're a traitor, Rob Williams, and if you think I'm going to tell you how to get along with your new girlfriend—"

His fingers clamped over my mouth, cutting off the rest of my tirade. "I don't want to get *along* with Reid—I want to get *rid* of her," Rob said desperately. "I wouldn't date her if she were the only girl on the planet! Now will you shut up and listen to me?"

I nodded. When his hand dropped to his side, I asked, "If you don't like her, why are you always hanging around her?"

"You know how much I love acting, and the plays Renee writes from Greek myths are really neat. But the biggest mistake I ever made in my life was agreeing to be in the Midas skit." He hunched his shoulders, confiding glumly, "Reid sticks to me like a wad of chewing gum. Since you're so sensitive and tactful, I thought you might be able to suggest a way to lose her without hurting her feelings."

A huge wave of relief made me giggle. "I don't think she

has any feelings, but just in case, when you're not rehearsing or horsing around with the guys, you can hang out with me," I offered. "The two of us can plan a welcome-back celebration for Lisa."

"I just got a letter from her, too."

"Won't it be fantastic to have her back at Alma?"

I returned his broad grin with one of my own. "You know it! Right after dinner, I'm going to write Mars and tell him the good news."

Dear Mars,

I'm so glad to hear that your leg is better. Do you think it'll be well enough for you to come back to Brighton a few days early next semester? I miss you a lot, and since we haven't had a chance to spend any time together this summer, it would be super if we could see each other before school starts.

Major Bulletin: Lisa's coming back to Alma! I spent a lot of time with Rob this afternoon and guess what? I think he's in love with her! He didn't exactly say so, but I could tell by the way he looked when he talked about her.

This has really been an up-and-down sort of day. I pulled a horrible boner with Maxie, but with a little help from Mr. Griffith, Amy, and Palmer, I think I can fix it. I'm planning to combine some of the shots I've taken into a music video of the Foxes' sizzling summer. I'm hoping that when Maxie sees it, she'll realize that she's very special to all of us.

I also passed the swimming test. In fact, Coach Barker says I may be good enough to make the team next fall. I doubt that I'll have time for it, though, because I'm planning to join Mr. G.'s camcorder club. It's been so much fun being the camp reporter that I'm thinking seriously of going into video journalism when I grow up.

Update on the baby-naming contest: Maggie and Dan announced that although there were a lot of good entries, they've decided to wait until after the baby is born to pick a name. (I suggested the names Margaret and Daniel, so that no matter how it turned out, we could call the kid Junior.) Everyone who entered is a winner, though—the Griffiths are going to host a pizza party at Figaro's after the christening, and we're all invited.

Aloha,
Shanon

P.S. I found out this evening that "aloha" is a Hawaiian word that can be used to say "hello," "good-bye," or "I love you." It's up to you to guess which way I mean it!

TIME CAPSULE ENTRY FIFTEEN: BY GEORGETTE DURAND

———◆———

Palmer has been quiet lately—much too quiet to suit me. In fact, after threatening to dump me in the lake, she hasn't said another mean thing to me. Either she really believed I'd made an honest mistake, or she was hatching some plot to get revenge. Knowing my stepsister, I tended to believe the second explanation.

Since there had been no reaction from Nikos, it was fairly safe to assume that he hadn't yet found the note. The only way I could escape this mess with all my body parts in working order was to get it back before he read it. But there was too much risk of being caught if I sneaked into his cabin and went through his knapsack in broad daylight. My plan was to hit the place on Talent Night while all the campers were at the amphitheater—and pray he didn't read it before then.

The morning of the show, I was understandably twitchy when Palmer breezed into rehearsal with a change in the skit.

"It just doesn't work for Midas to have two daughters— Georgette and I are tripping all over each other," she told

Renee. "Plus, we waste a lot of time changing into gold costumes after he zaps us. We're going to lose the audience's attention if we don't keep the action moving."

I knew she was right, but I wasn't about to let her bump me out of the play. "It's too late to change the script now," I said. Because I was already in hot water with her, I added, "From now on, I'll be more careful about hogging the spotlight."

"I wasn't really complaining about that," Palmer said, treating me to her sweetest smile. "The skit will flow much better if you play Marigold in the first part. Then the second Midas touches you, Renee will turn off the lights and you'll leave the stage. Then I'll come on and pose as Marigold the golden statue."

Renee's eyes widened with excitement. "That's brilliant!"

"Much more dramatic," Reid seconded grudgingly.

"But if we do it that way, you won't have much of a part, Palmer," Holbrook pointed out.

"I'll make that sacrifice to improve the production," she responded, letting out a long-suffering sigh.

It was totally out of character for my stepsister to settle for being a twenty-four-karat lawn ornament while I walked away with all of the lines! Right then and there, I knew she had something weird in mind.

For the rest of the day, my uneasiness continued to grow. By the time I put on my costume, my worry had developed into a full-blown anxiety attack.

"Where's Palmer?" I asked Reid, scanning the other performers in the girls' dressing room.

She added another layer of lipstick before she answered.

"She's coming late so no one will see her costume before she goes onstage."

That sounded ominous to me. "Do you know what she's wearing?"

"No, but I'll bet anything it's more spectacular than what you've got on," she replied.

I seriously doubted that. Costume-making materials were in short supply at Camp Emerald, and Palmer wasn't very good at do-it-yourself projects. I, on the other hand, was a genius at improvising. My ancient Greek costume was made from a pale blue tablecloth I'd snitched from the mess hall, and I'd spent hours in the craft center gluing a border of glitter around the bottom. With a scornful glance at the frumpy sheet Reid had pinned around her, I swept gracefully from the dressing room.

Amy was nearly finished with her performance when I reached the wings. Her voice sounded throatier than it had in rehearsal, and her moves were rock-star slick. The song she belted out—a funny satire she'd written about the boy-girl war—brought the house down.

The applause seemed to go on forever. Finally, after her third bow, Amy blew the crowd a kiss. I guess most everyone knew she aimed it at Nikos.

By now the rest of the Midas cast had assembled behind me, and as we waited for Maggie to introduce the skit, I was hit by a sudden attack of stage fright.

"Has Palmer come yet?" I whispered in panic to Holbrook.

He adjusted the gorilla costume he'd rigged from a bulky brown sweat suit and shook his head. "She'll make it on time," he predicted, squeezing my fingers. "Don't be nervous—you look so terrific that you're bound to be a smash."

It was surprising how much his compliment helped; when I stepped onstage for the first scene, my jitters had practically disappeared.

In our version of the Midas myth, Holbrook was a stray gorilla who'd followed Marigold home to the family's split-level suburban palace. "Please let me keep him, dear Father. This kind of ape is very rare," I begged, sinking dramatically to my knees in front of Rob.

Queen Reid, reeking of Jungle Muck, batted her eyes and wound her arms around her pretend-husband's neck. "Having a pet would teach the child responsibility, darling sweetums," she cooed, breathing heavily into Rob's ear.

According to the script, she was supposed to object because the gorilla would shed hairs all over the throne room. *Just what we need,* I thought. *She's ad-libbing her lines so she can get next to Rob.*

King Midas turned beet red. "Very well. If times get hard, we can always sell him to the zoo—or something," he said, sounding a little desperate. Rob clearly wasn't into ad-libbing.

The audience seemed to think it was all hilarious, and from then on, things got crazy. Reid trailed Rob around the stage closer than his shadow, not missing a single opportunity to plaster herself on him.

But Rob was more than a match for her. When the time came for him to test his new powers on the prop rose that was lying on the table, he whipped around and touched Reid's cheek instead.

"Quick thinking, Pops," I picked up his lead. "Since

140

mommie dearest can no longer move, you won't have to pay for the face-lift she needs so badly."

That broke the audience up, and as for Reid, she had no choice. She glared at us, but she had to hold the pose we'd tricked her into. Without her interference, we sailed on through the skit. Holbrook had the crowd rolling in the aisles. If there had been an Oscar for best performance by a gorilla, he would have won hands down.

Everything was going so smoothly that we were only seconds away from Palmer's entrance, when I realized she still hadn't appeared in the wings. She was definitely up to something, but the only thing I could do was go on with my lines.

"Please don't harm my ape, Father," I pleaded.

"Get real, Daughter. With gold at an all-time high, your hairy friend will bring a zillion dollars on the open market," Rob said, lunging at Holbrook.

At the last minute I shielded my pet with my own body. Rob's fingers closed around my arm and I screamed, "Ouch—I can feel myself turning into goollldddd!"

Renee cut the lights right on cue, and a second later I heard Palmer whisper, "Move it, kid—the real star has arrived."

I'd scarcely reached the wings when a gasp from the audience spun me around.

Palmer was in the spotlight, arms held above her head with the grace of a prima ballerina, head tilted regally toward Rob. She was wearing a sequined bikini that was skimpy enough to get her banned from quite a few beaches. But it was neither the pose nor the swimsuit that held everyone spellbound—it was her skin. From head to toe,

141

every square inch of my stepsister had been spray-painted a dazzling metallic gold!

The crowd went wild—particularly the guys. Whistling, cheering, and screaming held up the performance for a good five minutes, and all that time, Palmer was as still as if she had actually been turned into a statue.

I thought she was attempting a curtsy when she took a step forward. But she rocked back and forth a little, as though she were dizzy, and then collapsed in a heap on the floor. Needless to say, that was the end of the skit.

Renee immediately dropped the curtain. Everyone in the cast was too shocked to move, so Maggie was first to reach the middle of the stage. She touched Palmer's shoulder, and some of the gold rubbed off on her hand. "This isn't body paint. Where did you get it, Palmer?" the teacher queried sharply.

"From a cabinet in the art room." Palmer gulped, shaking her head groggily. "I guess the fumes got to me when I sprayed it on, but I'll be okay as soon as I get some fresh air."

Maggie was grim as she helped Palmer to her feet. "That stuff could prevent oxygen from getting to your skin."

"You mean I might suffocate?" Palmer squeaked.

"Not if we get it off immediately. Go straight to my cabin and park yourself in the tub. I'll be there as soon as I round up some nontoxic solvent."

As Maggie hurried away, I found the robe Palmer had worn before she made her grand entrance. "I'll go with you and help scrub off the paint. You're going to be okay," I assured her, draping the terry-cloth robe around her shining body. Before I could stop myself, I asked, "Why would you do a dumb thing like spraying yourself gold?"

142

"It's all your fault. You're a better actress than I am, so I had to do something spectacular to get the audience's attention." Scowling, she jerked away from me. "Just leave me alone."

The accusation didn't faze me a bit—I was used to getting blamed for stuff that was her fault. Certain that Maggie and a little turpentine would take care of the problem, I slipped out of the side of the amphitheater to retrieve Palmer's note. The talent show was due to run for another half hour, so I wasn't particularly pressed as I headed for the boys' side of camp. Unfortunately, I hadn't thought to bring a flashlight, and I had to snap on the overhead lamp when I walked into the cabin Nikos shared with Paul, Rob, John, and Holbrook.

I'd never been in an all-boys' room before, and quite naturally I was curious. Much to my disappointment, the guys' place was as junky as ours. It didn't take long to locate Nikos's knapsack; I plopped down on one of the bunks to go through it, first helping myself to some trail mix that was on the table.

Bingo! I found Palmer's note still tucked in the side pocket of the pouch—I was now officially off the hook.

"What are you doing?" Nikos's voice cut through my silent celebration.

My mouth dropped open, but nothing would come out.

Frowning suspiciously, he strode across the room and tweaked the paper from my shaking fingers. "I'm not the least bit interested in your sister. Why does she keep coming on to me?" he growled after he read the note. "Did she make you deliver this?"

I shook my head, and when I finally located my missing

voice, I stammered, "I wasn't delivering it, I was trying to get it back. It doesn't belong to you."

"Then why does it start, 'Dear N.S.'?"

"That stands for, er—Neato Sugarplum," I supplied. It was bad, but it was the only thing I could think of at the moment. "It's Palmer's pet name for her secret pen pal. They've been writing each other ever since camp started, and I usually deliver the mail. Only this time, I got mixed up and stuck it in your knapsack instead of his."

His expression was disbelieving, but some of the hostility was gone. "Why do they write when they can see each other every day?"

"Uh—Neato and Palmer are too shy to talk to each other in person," I said, arranging my features into a picture of earnest innocence. "The other day when Palmer met you in the woods, she wasn't coming on to you at all. She really wanted to ask you to help them get together, but you never gave her a chance to explain that."

He apparently bought it, because his mouth eased into a smile. "I don't usually go in for fixing other people up, but since Palmer is Amy's roommate, I might make an exception. You'll have to tell me who Neato Sugarplum is, though."

Totally trapped in my own web of lies, I closed my eyes and blurted out the first name that popped into my head.

TIME CAPSULE
ENTRY SIXTEEN:
BY PALMER DURAND

Dear Palmer,

Just a note to let you know I'm back from Europe. I had a terrific time, especially in France. While I was walking down the Champs-Elysées, I spotted a pretty blonde who looked very familiar. I ran a couple of blocks to catch up with her, and when I did, I was very disappointed to see that she wasn't Palmer Durand!

After I got back to the States, I went down to Palm Beach to visit my grandparents. When I phoned your house, your mother gave me your address. If you had told me you were going to camp, I would have sent you a bunch of postcards.

Hope you're having fun this summer. Maybe we'll get to see each other during the holidays.

All the best,
Rain Blackburn

It wasn't exactly a love letter, but it was the closest I'd gotten to romance all summer. And it proved to me that there was real potential in my relationship with Rain: The fact that he'd keep my Palm Beach number meant that he liked me. Plus, he'd sent a picture of himself standing in front of the Eiffel Tower. I'd carry that snapshot with me as long as I lived. Which could be a very short time; in less than ten minutes, the bus would be leaving for the site of our camp's survival weekend.

"I just know this is going to be terrific," Georgette bubbled, her gaze skidding over the crowd of campers surrounding us.

I could tell from the glazed look in her eyes that she was as twitchy as I was—usually we both tried to avoid going one-on-one with Mother Nature. "About as much fun as a dentist appointment," I answered.

The fake enthusiasm faded from her expression and she peered at me worriedly. "Your skin looks a little blotchy."

"What with all that scrubbing after the skit, it's a wonder I have any left."

"It was a horrible experience for you," my stepsister sympathized, pulling a snapshot from her pocket. "One of the guys backstage took this with a Polaroid—I thought you might like to have it for a souvenir. I didn't get to tell you last night, but you really looked good."

Good didn't begin to describe my image—it was absolutely spectacular! "This is not bad," I said, smiling modestly. "I'll send it to Rain when I answer his letter."

"I'm so glad you heard from him. The photograph he sent was to die for—he's a lot better-looking than Nikos," she sighed. "While we're on the subject, I got your note back last night."

"Was it still in the knapsack? Do you think he had a chance to read it?"

146

"Yes and yes," she answered. "He caught me red-handed, but he bought my alibi. Now will you forgive me for interfering in your business?"

"That depends. What did you say to Nikos?"

"I'll tell you when we get on the bus—it's a long story."

Before I could get any more information, Mr. Griffith stepped to the front of the crowd and waved his arms to get our attention.

"I hope you all enjoyed breakfast this morning, because for the next two days, you'll be eating K rations and whatever we manage to find in the wilderness," he began.

There was a chorus of groans that included one from me. Roots and twigs were dead last on my list of edible items.

"This weekend isn't about fun, it's about survival, and that's serious business," he warned. "Remember, this is strictly a voluntary exercise. If anyone isn't comfortable with it, feel free not to go. The rest of you can start loading your gear."

A few kids—one of them Reid Olivier—edged away from the pack and headed for the Trading Post. Georgette and I exchanged a wistful glance.

"If you're afraid, I'd be glad to stay here with you. We could spend the weekend giving each other cosmetic makeovers and planning our fall wardrobes," she suggested.

The offer was more than tempting, but I shook my head. "Durands don't wimp out," I said firmly. Since she'd cleaned up the Nikos mess, I figured she was due a little sisterly affection. "Stick close to me, kid. I won't let anything bad happen to you."

"Got a minute, Palmer?" Nikos walked over to ask.

"There's something I have to say to you before we get on the bus."

"You two will have to excuse me—I've got to go find Renee," Georgette gulped, skittering away.

I could feel myself turning red, so I ducked my head to study the gold paint that still clung to the rims of my nails. "What's on your mind, Nikos?" I mumbled.

"I want to apologize for the way I acted when I ran into you on the trail"—he jammed his hands in his pockets of his shorts and continued—"and for thinking you were a conceited, selfish airhead. I'm sorry I misjudged you—you're a very special human being."

"Really?" I glanced up warily—there wasn't even a hint of sarcasm in his expression.

Nikos studied me anxiously before he went on, "I hope this isn't embarrassing you. Georgette told me how shy you are."

Shy? I bit my bottom lip to keep from laughing. "I'm working hard to get over it," I murmured, chalking up two points for Georgette. "Hearing nice things about myself helps."

"Some girls only care about the way a guy looks or how much money his family has. It's great to know you're not like that."

"I've always believed that the inside of a person is more important than the outside," I agreed modestly. "Do go on."

"That's about all I have to say, except to wish you and Neato Sugarplum good luck. He's a terrific guy, isn't he?"

"The best," I stammered, totally confused.

"There's Amy—I've got to cut out now." Nikos

bounded off, calling back, "Neato is saving you a seat on the bus."

It took me a minute to find Georgette and ten seconds to haul her off to the edge of the crowd. "Exactly what did you tell Nikos Smith?"

She turned pale and launched into a garbled story about her raid on the boys' cabin. Halfway through, I tightened my grip on her arm. "Cough up, sister dear. Who's Neato Sugarplum?"

Georgette swallowed hard. "Holbrook Wellington."

My whole world dropped out from under me. When word about me riding to the survival weekend beside Holbrook hit Ardsley's campus, my dating stock would be worth zilch.

I was reaching for Georgette's throat when Mr. Griffith ordered everyone onto the bus. Georgette jerked away from my grasp and scurried off.

I waited until the very last minute to board. Gritting my teeth, I prepared myself for laughter, hoots, ridicule—anything but the applause that broke out as I turned to confront the passengers.

Rob Williams jumped up from his place beside Shanon to lead off the chant, "Pal-mer, Pal-mer, Pal-mer," and a banner that read "CAMP EMERALD'S GOLDEN GIRL" was stretched above the rear window. When I started down the aisle, kids on either side bounced up and down, applauding.

By the time I reached the seat Holbrook had saved for me, my face was fire-engine red with embarrassment, but I'd never been more delighted in my entire life.

"I hope you like the sign I made," he mumbled shyly as I sat down beside him.

"It's super. When I go back to school, I'm going to hang it in my room," I promised, feeling terribly guilty for the way I'd been using him. "Holbrook, there's something I have to tell you—"

"Georgette's already explained the whole thing," he interrupted. He leaned closer to whisper, "This morning I talked to Nikos and backed up your cover story. I told him that you'd been writing to me because you've a very kind person, not because you're romantically interested in me."

A sudden lump rose in my throat; no one was more surprised than I was when I leaned over to plant a kiss on his cheek. "Holbrook Wellington, you really are a Neato Sugarplum."

TIME CAPSULE
ENTRY SEVENTEEN:
BY AMY HO

Being a roller-coaster freak, I should have enjoyed the bus ride to Franconia Notch, the site of the survival exercise. The route we took was two hours worth of unbelievably steep grades, hair-raising curves, stomach-lurching drops, and the most awesome scenery in New England. I hardly glanced at the passing view, though, because I spent a lot of the trip in a blue fog.

The one big item on my worry list was Palmer. Her favorite sport was boy-snatching, and lately she'd been sending out definite signals that she was interested in Nikos. I'd ignored the vibes because I was positive he was Palmer-proof. Most of the time we'd been at camp, he had acted as though he couldn't stand my roommate. But that was before Talent Night. When I spotted them having a cozy chat before we got on the bus, I was sure I was history; how could I possibly compete with Camp Emerald's Golden Girl?

Although Nikos and I shared a seat, he hardly said two words to me during the whole ride. In fact, he was acting decidedly weird—one minute he was hyper and fidgety, the next stony and aloof. By the time we reached the top of the mountain his seesaw routine was definitely beginning to grate on my nerves. He was on the upside of the cycle when he climbed off the bus. As we headed for the campers clustered around Mr. Griffith, Nikos walked—correction, *swaggered*—two paces in front of me, the bulk of his shoulders straining against his T-shirt. Was he trying to impress Palmer with his biceps? I wondered miserably. I didn't have much time to brood about it, though, because Mr. G. was already leading the group toward the spot where the climbing tests would take place. I fell in step with Shanon and we tried to look like we weren't uneasy about what was coming up.

The first exercise wasn't too horrible. Ten feet above the ground, a long line was stretched tightly between two oaks; we were supposed to start in tree number one, swing hand over hand along the rope to tree number two, then climb down again.

Shanon groaned. "I'll never be able to do that!"

"Yes, you will. You'll be wearing a safety harness so you can't possibly get hurt," I told her. "If your arms get tired before you make it to the platform, just let go. It'll only be a five-foot drop to the ground."

"Good advice," Mr. Griffith said. "Would you like to have the first shot at it, Amy?"

Before I could open my mouth to answer, Nikos bounded to the head of the pack. Without bothering with the safety harness, he shinnied up the first oak in nothing flat and launched himself onto the taut rope. His body swung effortlessly through the air. Halfway across, he freed one hand to wave to all of us who were gaping up at him. He made it to the other tree in under thirty seconds, but instead of climbing down, executed a neat midair somersault and landed on his feet. He waited until the applause died down, then he pounded his chest with his fists and let out a Tarzan yodel of triumph.

"Show-off," I muttered under my breath.

"You've just failed the first exercise, Smith," said Mr. G. as Nikos rejoined the group. "From here on out, anyone who ignores safety procedures won't be allowed to participate in the exercises."

I shot Nikos a smug look, sprinted for the first tree, and hooked myself into the harness.

My time was nearly as good as Nikos's. In fact, I would have beaten him if the tail of my T-shirt hadn't snagged on a slab of bark. When I reached the ground again, Mr. G. guided me over to stand beside Nikos. "If you two want to compete, you can sit on the bus and play checkers until the rest of us finish the course," he lectured. "The only way to survive in the wilderness is to cooperate. You got that?"

"Yessir," we said in unison.

When he had gone to supervise the rest of the crossings, Nikos sneaked a sidelong glance at me. "There's something I need to talk to you about, Amy."

I could feel a brush-off coming. Determined to take it without batting an eyelash, I snapped out a tight, "What is it?"

He looked at me for a long moment, then dropped his gaze to the ground. "Nothing important. Race you to the next test," he challenged, dashing away.

There was no doubt in my mind that the second exercise had been designed by a maniac! In the middle of a clearing there was a tall wooden wall; since it was studded with metal brackets that resembled staples, it didn't take much

153

for us to figure out we were supposed to climb to the narrow platform on top.

"What happens once we get up there?" Palmer asked warily.

Mr. Griffith gestured toward a trapeze that was suspended from an overhanging limb of a nearby tree. "You dive out and catch the bar," he explained.

By my calculations, the trapeze was a very long stretch from the platform and a healthy fifteen feet above the ground. Even the fact that we would be strapped in a harness that was attached to safety lines didn't do much to reassure me.

"I'm afraid of heights, Mr. G.," Holbrook said, backing off immediately.

"Then don't push yourself. Just relax and sit this one out." Mr. G. turned to Palmer, asking, "Think you're up to this one?"

Her eyes went glassy, but to her credit she dragged herself toward the wall. Three handholds up, she peeked over her shoulder, gave a dainty "Eeeek," then scrambled to the ground.

The smattering of applause that greeted her descent was led by none other than Nikos Smith.

"What's the big deal?" I asked. "My five-year-old cousin could have done better than that."

Nikos shrugged. "Climbing isn't easy for—"

"A girl?" I cut in.

"*That* girl," he corrected with a grin. "You'd never think Palmer could climb wearing that fancy sportswear."

Great. Now he was impressed with her clothes. Just one more clue that I was on my way out.

"Amy, would you hold this while I take my turn?" Shanon handed me her camcorder. "Better still, film my climb. I want Mars to have something to remember me by if I don't make it."

Giggling nervously, she scurried to the wall and strapped herself into the harness. It took ten minutes of tape for her to reach the platform. My zoom close-up caught the trembling in her legs and a stressed-out expression on her face. As scared as she obviously was, though, she didn't give up until she was standing at the top. She smiled as we all cheered, but then called out, "I can't make the jump."

"That was a super job, Shanon," said Mr. G. "Take it slow and easy on the way back down."

Of the next ten campers that followed, only Maxie, Paul, and John Adams managed to leap toward the trapeze. Max and Paul almost made it, but my ex–pen pal missed the bar by a country mile. It gave me a good deal of satisfaction to see John Adams being lowered to the ground by way of the safety line.

"Tough luck, John," I murmured as he stalked past me.

"I'd like to see you do any better."

"Oh, you will," I promised.

Nikos and I were the last in line, and when our turns came, he gave me a mocking, "Ladies first."

"Someone's got to show you how," I agreed.

"Forget it," he said through gritted teeth as he started to climb.

Nikos's performance was a thing of beauty, each movement graced with style and power. He reached the platform with very little effort, and as he stood poised for his dive, a stray breeze whipped his hair into a dark halo around his face. The scene seemed to switch into slow motion. He floated out into space, his fingers stretching

155

toward the trapeze. As his hands grasped the bar, his head turned toward me, and he smiled. Right then and there, I knew that I loved him. The warm feeling that swept over me was all the more reason I had to do my best. If I turned in an excellent performance on the trapeze, maybe Nikos would forget Palmer's sequined bikini!

It took a lot longer for me to reach the top of the wooden wall than it had taken Nikos. The palms of my hands were so slick with sweat that I kept losing my grip on the brackets. When I finally got to the platform, I stared at the trapeze, burning its position into my brain. I didn't have much control over my leap; fear buckled my legs and I sort of toppled over the edge.

My eyelids were fighting me all the way: the harder I tried to keep them open, the tighter they stayed shut. I waved my arms blindly—whoever was watching over lovesick idiots that day must've been on the job, because by some miracle, my fingers locked around the bar of the trapeze!

Below me everyone was cheering like crazy. But when Mr. G. lowered me to the ground, Nikos Smith was staring off into space as though he hadn't even watched.

"You were terrific," Nikos said absently when I reached him.

I didn't even get the chance for a sarcastic comeback because Mr. G. called everyone together.

"Listen up, gang," he began. "I've been conducting these survival exercises for three years now, and this is by far the best group I've ever had. I knew you'd do well, so I had Mrs. Butter bake a couple of chocolate cakes to go with your K-ration dinners. They're waiting for you on the other side of the mountain."

Holbrook glanced back at the sheer face of the cliff behind us, his cheeks going pale. "If it's all the same to you, Mr. Griffith, I'll skip dessert today. There's no way in the world I can make it up those rocks."

"Not to worry—we're going *through* the mountain, not over it," Mr. G. assured him. As Mr. Griffith led us toward an outcropping of stones at the base of the cliff, he issued our marching orders: "Stay close together, kids. The mountain is honeycombed with tunnels. Most of them have been explored, and the ones that lead to the outside are marked with green circles. If you should happen to get separated from the group, though, keep away from the shafts that have red squares painted on the walls. Those tunnels are dead ends."

"You probably shouldn't say 'dead' to people who're about to go underground," Maxie joked uneasily, moving closer to Paul.

"Will there be bats, Mr. Griffith?" Georgette squeaked in a very small voice.

"Not in the main corridors. This is not going to be nearly as scary as you think, guys. You've all got flashlights, and once you get adjusted to being inside, I think you're going to like it."

I thought I heard Nikos say, "Fat chance," but when I glanced at him, his lips were pressed together in a thin line. His skin appeared to be a shade paler, and there was a slight sheen of perspiration on his forehead.

"Are you okay?" I asked.

"Why shouldn't I be?" he mumbled, kneeling to retie his shoelaces. By the time he straightened up, most of the other kids had gone on ahead of us.

When people answer my question with another question, I generally suspect them of hiding something. But I figured pressing Nikos wouldn't do much good, so I kept my mouth shut and joined the back of the single-file line now going into the cave. Nikos fell in behind me.

The entrance was low and narrow, and there was a chill, moist feel to the air inside. I wasn't exactly crazy about the place, but when we all snapped on our flashlights, it was beautiful in an alien sort of way. Past the first corridor, we hung a left and moved into an awesome cavern. The limestone formations hanging from the ceiling reminded me of icicles. A couple of turns later, Mr. G. pointed out ancient Indian drawings on the wall.

"Isn't this neat?" I asked Nikos.

There was no answer. And when I trained my beam on the spot beside me, there was no Nikos.

My immediate suspicion was that he'd gone to be with Palmer. But she, Georgette, Renee, and Holbrook were bunched together near Mr. Griffith. A quick look ahead told me that Nikos wasn't with Shanon, Rob, or John, either. When I turned to peer back, I saw a light bobbing along the way we had already come.

Instinct made me turn to follow Nikos. He was moving pretty fast, and by the time I caught up with him, he was back in the icicle room.

"Why did you leave the group?" I asked.

"I've got to get out of here."

I was totally exasperated. "I'll bet you're looking for a shortcut so you can beat everybody else to the other side of the mountain. Why do you always have to be first?"

"It's not that." He swallowed as though his mouth were very dry. "I'm afraid."

My jaw dropped and I did a double take. "You what?"

"I've had claustrophobia ever since I was a little kid. Being in places like this makes me feel like I can't breathe," he admitted, not looking at me. "All day long I've been pumping myself up to handle this, but I can't. I tried to tell you before, but I was afraid you'd think I was a wimp."

"If you were a wimp, you wouldn't have rescued me from the wasps. And anyway—" I stopped abruptly, hit by a flash of insight: Fear of going into the cave was the reason he'd been acting strange all morning. Relief made me blurt out, "I thought you wanted to talk to me about Palmer!"

"What could I possibly have to say about her?" Nikos's breath was coming in short gasps now. "If I don't get outside pretty soon, I'm going to do something really stupid—like scream or faint!"

I slipped my hand in his and squeezed his fingers. "It's okay—I'm in this with you, and it won't take long for us to catch up with the others."

That was easier said than done. There were lots of corridors leading from the icicle room, and for the life of me, I couldn't remember which one we'd taken before. I began to get scared when I realized that we were alone in a maze with nothing between us and total darkness but our flashlights. What would we do if our batteries failed? Especially considering that Nikos's terror had to be a zillion times more intense than mine.

"Plan B—we follow the green circles on the walls," I suggested, remembering Mr. G.'s earlier instructions. Common sense told me that if I could keep Nikos's mind off our predicament, he'd have a better shot at controlling his panic. As we moved from corridor to corridor, searching for the green circles, I eased into a discussion of the chat he'd had with Palmer.

The story he said Georgette had told him sounded extremely weird. It had to be that one of Palmer's schemes had gone sour and she was using her stepsister as a cover. But the notion that my roommate could be romantically attracted to Holbrook was the hoot of the year! At the moment, though, the only thing I really cared about was that Nikos was not one bit interested in Palmer Durand.

I guess my diversion tactics worked because as we wandered through the cave Nikos's voice started sounding more normal, and his hand stopped shaking. Even as I realized it, he dropped my fingers and slipped his arm around my shoulders.

"For what it's worth, I'd like to apologize for taking you out of the softball game when you had a no-hitter going. I'm also sorry if that underwear thing embarrassed you. I tried to tell John not to . . ."

When his sentence trailed off, I raised my light so I could get a better look at his expression. "John Adams planned the panty raid?"

Nikos nodded. "Don't be too hard on him, though. He's jealous because you and I have been spending so much time together."

"Why should he care what we do?"

"Because he's still crazy about you."

That nearly blew me away. "I always thought that John and I were just good buddies. I never thought that he liked me—that way."

We walked in silence for a while, then Nikos's arm tightened around me. "Did you know that I like you—that way?"

160

"I do now. And while we're into 'show and tell,' I like you—that way, too," I confessed softly. For a minute I thought the glow from my happiness was magically lifting the gloom from the cavern. But then I spotted a patch of sunlight shining though an opening in the rocks up ahead. "We're almost there, Nikos."

Just before we reached the exit from the cave, Nikos came to a stop.

"I thought you needed to get out in the fresh air," I said, puzzled.

"There's something I have to do before we leave."

He retrieved his pocketknife, and opening the blade, he began to carve deep lines in the stone wall. After a few strokes, the initials A.H. and N.S. began to take shape. When he had finished, I borrowed his knife and drew a lopsided heart around the letters.

Nikos gently touched my cheek. "Mr. G. was right— cooperation is a heck of a lot better than competition."

161

TIME CAPSULE
ENTRY EIGHTEEN:
BY SHANON DAVIS

Dear Mars,

It's amazing how fast three weeks can go by. Tomorrow is the last full day we'll have at Emerald Lake. I think camp has been good for the Foxes of the Third Dimension. We've all had a lot of ups and downs, but as usual there have been more good times than bad. The important thing is that we're still the best of friends.

I've got to run now because Mr. Griffith, Amy, and Palmer are waiting to help me put the finishing touches on my music videotape. I hope it convinces Maxie that she's as much my friend as Lisa. I'll let you know how it turns out in my next letter.

> *Hugs, kisses, and get-well wishes,*
> *Shanon*

The plan was coming together beautifully. Thanks to Georgette and Renee, the TV room in the rec center was decorated with crepe paper and balloons. (They'd gotten up an hour before reveille to do the job.) The popcorn was popped, the sodas were cold, and in exactly five and a half minutes, Paul would be escorting Maxie through the door.

I glanced at my watch, so nervous that I could hardly focus on the numbers. "What could be keeping the guys?" I asked crossly.

"They had a little run to make," Palmer answered, her mouth curving in a mysterious smile.

"They'll be here in plenty of time." Amy tuned a string on her guitar, watching out of the corner of her eye as I headed for the television with a paper towel. "You've already cleaned the screen fifteen times, Shanon. Chill out, will you?"

I fiddled with the dials on the VCR. "I just want everything to be perfect."

"Mission accomplished," Nikos said, winking at Amy from the doorway. He strolled in with Rob and Holbrook close on his heels.

"What mission?" I asked.

"Just guy stuff," Rob supplied, grinning. He came over to plop a party hat on my head. "How does it feel to be a brilliant young producer/director?"

"Weird. I've got butterflies the size of Texas in my stomach."

Just then our lookouts, Georgette and Renee, dashed into the room giggling. "They're coming!"

Holbrook hit the lights and we all scrambled for cover.

"But I don't want to watch TV. I'd much rather go swimming," Maxie protested as Paul dragged her into the darkened room. "Who needs an educational special in the middle of the summer?"

"Trust me—you're going to love it," he promised, clicking on the light switch.

"SURPRISE!!" we all yelled in unison.

Maxie's face went blank with shock. "It's not my birthday."

"Yes it is—sort of." I moved over to take her arm. "You're the new star who's about to be born."

My audience settled down on the cushions in front of the TV, but as I headed for the VCR, Nikos intercepted me.

"I've got it covered. Park yourself and enjoy the show," he ordered firmly. After I took my place with the other Foxes, he slipped the separate sound track Amy had recorded into the cassette player and turned on my video.

S.D. Studios Presents
"Foxes Unlimited"
Starring: Maxie Schloss, Amy Ho,
Palmer Durand, Shanon Davis, and
Lisa McGreevy.
Cameo appearances by: Junior
Foxettes Georgette Durand and
Renee Quick.
Special Guests Stars: The fantastic
Ardie Pen Pals.

After the credits, still photos of me and my suitemates flashed onto the screen. The shot of Lisa—the only time she appeared on the tape—was from a snapshot I carried in my wallet.

For the next fifteen minutes, we went through a collage of our summer: Maxie and Paul eating hot dogs in front of the campfire; Amy before and after her encounter with the wasps; Palmer, sleek and shining in her gold skin and sequined bikini. There was even a shot of me standing petrified on top of the trapeze platform.

While my main storyline had been the friendship among the Foxes, the strong subplot was romance. Knowing how easily embarrassed Maxie and Paul were, I'd been very careful not to include sequences of them holding hands.

Three quarters of the way through the show, everyone was having a ball—except me. I was just getting more and more depressed. Both my tape and my summer had omitted something very, very important—Mars Martinez. It was so unfair that we had missed being together in this beautiful place.

I must have done a pretty fair job with the production, because when THE END flickered onto the screen, the applause was loud and long.

"I got your message loud and clear, Shanon," Maxie said, wrapping her arms around me. "You're a very special friend."

Amy and Palmer joined in on the group hug, but when it was over, I burst into tears.

"What's wrong?" Max asked anxiously.

I couldn't stop crying long enough to tell her how much I missed Mars.

"You look like you could use one of these." A boy's arm reached from behind to drop a box of tissues in my lap.

I pulled one out and blew hard. "Thanks, Mars."

MARS?

He was really there, standing right behind me, cast and crutches included! And the smile on his face was the biggest, sweetest one I'd ever seen him wear.

It took a full minute before my vocal cords would work, but when I finally got them together, I couldn't make them stop. "When did you get here? How long can you stay? Why didn't you tell me you were coming? How's your leg? Oh, Mars, I'm so glad to see you!"

"This morning. Overnight—I'm going to ride back on the bus with you tomorrow. Because I wanted to surprise you. The cast comes off in three weeks," he answered my questions in order, holding me tightly. "And I'm glad to see you, too."

When it finally occurred to me that we were hugging each other in broad daylight with everybody watching, I turned red and backed away from him. "How did you manage to pull this off?" I asked.

"Dad had business to take care of in Concord, and I bugged him until he said he'd drop me off here," Mars explained. Grinning, he brushed away one of my tears. "We don't have much time left, so please don't waste any more of it crying."

"Right," I snuffled. "I'll go wash my face."

"Good move. Crying makes you puffy," Palmer agreed, surveying me with a dismayed frown. Signaling Amy and Maxie to follow, she guided me toward the door with a brisk "It's going to take a lot of work to whip you into shape."

"Hurry back, Shanon," Mars called after us.

In less than fifteen minutes I was decked out in one of Palmer's chic playsuits, Amy had twisted my hair into a new, mod look—pinning it with her lucky barrette for good measure—and Maxie, of all people, was giving me advice on kissing techniques!

"Thanks, guys—it doesn't get any better than this," I said. I was so happy I had to hug myself to keep from exploding.

Before I left the cabin, though, there was one last thing I had to do. Pulling my notebook from under a pile of clothes on the desk, I scribbled a hurried note:

Dear Time Capsule Reader,

As you've probably guessed by now, this is the last of our entries. Since you know the scoop on Maxie and Paul and Amy and Nikos, I didn't think it was quite fair to leave you without a few words about me and Mars.

It's going to be hard to squeeze three whole weeks into one day, but I'm going to give it my very best shot. His cast automatically eliminates canoe rides, romantic walks, and moonlight swims (let's not get crazy—I'm not that good, yet). So maybe we'll just find a quiet spot down by the lake where we can sit and talk to each other. And if the stars are out tonight—who knows? I may even work up enough courage to tell Mars that I love him.

Yours truly,
Shanon Davis

Something to write home about . . .

another new Pen Pals story!

In Book 18, DOUBLE DATE, Lisa's back at the Alma Stephens School for Girls! But she's not the same Lisa who left a year ago—she's more outgoing than ever and she isn't used to playing by the rules. After the Foxes stumble upon the empty country mansion of a movie star, Lisa talks Palmer into sneaking back to the house for a secret meeting with their pen pals. The plan sounds perfect, and the girls are totally excited. But getting caught could turn their dream date into a nightmare . . .

GUESS WHAT?
PEN PALS BARBARA AND JENNIFER
GOT THEIR NAMES IN A PEN PALS BOOK!

Pen Pals Barbara Goldman from Durham, North Carolina, and Jennifer Wright, from Portland, Oregon, *both* wrote to us—about how they're writing to each other! Barbara and Jennifer write to each other so often that sometimes their letters cross in the mail. What they'd like to do more than anything else in the world is attend the same camp next summer, just like the characters in this book!

Congratulations, Barbara and Jennifer! Check out pages 69, 70, and 73 of Super Special #2: Summer Sizzle and you will see that characters have been named after you. Barbara and Jennifer play softball with Amy and Nikos on a team called The Avengers.

Don't thank us, Barbara and Jennifer. Thank Sharon Dennis Wyeth for making your names famous!

Every month, Sharon Dennis Wyeth, the author of the PEN PALS series, names a character in one of her books after a PEN PALS reader. If you'd like to have a character named after you, write in and let us know what's going on with you and your pen pal. What do you guys actually *say* in your letters? Are you making any exciting plans to call or visit your pen pals?

Don't write back soon, write now! Send your letters to:

PEN PALS HEADQUARTERS
c/o PARACHUTE PRESS
156 FIFTH AVE. ROOM 325
NEW YORK, NY 10010

People *really do* get Pen Pals! Why don't you get one, too? Fill out the form on the next page and let us find you a fun new friend!

169

WANTED: BOYS — AND GIRLS —
WHO CAN WRITE !

Join the Pen Pals Exchange and get a pen pal of your own!

Fill out the form below.

Send it with a self-addressed stamped envelope to:

PEN PALS EXCHANGE
c/o The Trumpet Club
PO Box 632
Holmes, PA 19043
U.S.A.

In a couple of weeks you'll receive the name and address of someone who wants to be your pen pal.

Cut here --

PEN PALS EXCHANGE

NAME _____ GRADE _____

ADDRESS _____

TOWN _____ STATE _____ ZIP _____

DON'T FORGET TO INCLUDE A STAMPED ENVELOPE WITH YOUR NAME AND ADDRESS ON IT!

Please check one

☐ I bought this book in a store.

☐ I bought this book through the Trumpet Book Club.

Look for your name in PEN PALS books. We'll pick names of matched up Pen Pals every month to print right in a PEN PALS book.